REBELLION

THE DEPARTURE   BOOK I   VOL. I

MASON ALLAN

To Raymond

All the best.

Mason Allan

ISBN: 978-1-7331028-0-3

Dedicated to all decent human beings who try their best
in this world of ours
and to every child who's dreamed of being super

Acknowledgements

This novel, short though it may be, is the product of over five years of dreaming, working, writing, learning, and brainstorming. As such, it is the beneficiary of tremendous help, support, and aid from friends, family, mentors, and kind strangers, many of whom I haven't the memory to thank at this time. If one such individual is reading this and discovers that they were left out, I'm sorry. There are more books to come, so I'll make sure to acknowledge you in at least one of them.

Firstly, I must thank my editor Cynthia Merrill, who was a dream to work with. Many thanks to Jeffery Wolf, Mari Molen, Cameron Hopkin, and Erica Smith, the members of the Sanderson Crew, as well as Dane Whitaker and Matt Wagstaff. All of you contributed to this novel, and it is a product of your feedback, to some degree.

Thanks are due to my army of friends who have supported the writing of this novel as well. Colin Stuart, Stephen Bickel, Derek Bethers, Weber Griffiths, Maggie Gunn, Riley Johnson, David Belnap, Shannon Lyman, Katy Smith, Conner Olsen, Alec Martin, and many others have all waited years for this book.

I would also like to thank the many teachers and professors who have taught me over the years and who have helped show me that the world is filled with interesting information and powerful knowledge, too much for any one person to contain. I would particularly like to thank Monica Richards, John Bennion, Joey Franklin, Peter Leman, Trent Hickman, Elise Moberly, Gideon Burton, and Brandon Sanderson for making my college experience one of good memories and growth. However, I'd also like to thank Julie Gardner, Matt Barnes, Paul Walstead, Angela Van Berckelaer, and a legion of others who made a lasting impact on my personal intellectual expansion. Finally, I'd like to thank the teachers who helped me in elementary school. I was energetic, unfocused, and disorganized, and I got myself into plenty of less-than-advantageous scholastic situations. The compassion they showed me is something I am still grateful for today.

Lastly, I need to thank my family, since it is their lifelong support, generosity, and love that made this book possible. They've encouraged me on my way to my dreams, despite how hare-brained they may sometimes be and despite how hopeless I sometimes am. Thank you,

Lucy, Molly, Porter, Madi, and Brynley and, above all else, thanks, Mom and Dad. You're all too good to me.

1

Clay

Clayton Moore didn't wake up believing he'd change the world.

He sat in bed, embraced only by cheap bedsheets and the semi-darkness of his Seattle apartment. The fluorescent lighting of the city outside pierced the battered blinds that tried, and failed, to cover his bedroom window. The room's cool temperature easily seeped through his thin cocoon of cloth.

He hadn't slept much but, then again, he rarely did. He'd had a tough time sleeping for years, now. Even before he'd infiltrated the city, his nightmares had regularly derailed any peace generally hoped for at night. Then the assassination attempts had started once he'd arrived in Seattle and gotten a job with the City Guard. Sleep was something of an uncommon commodity on any regular night.

Today, however, was anything but regular, because today was the day.

He repositioned himself, sheets rustling as he shifted and glanced at his alarm clock. The ball of metal hovered next to his bed, standing on thin air as its blazing numbers declared to the dark room that it was nine minutes past six in the morning. He had precisely 21 minutes left before he had to arise, still sleep-deprived and groggy, from his stiff mattress. Exhaustion plagued his limbs, making them limp and weak, tempting him to remain in the confines of his bed, but that wasn't an option. He took a deep breath, pushing against the stress that pushed against him.

Hang in there, man, he thought. *Just make it through the day.*

He scooped up the hologram-projector resting on the dirty floor near his bed. Clay didn't own a table, or it'd be resting there. The projector was a handy thing. The small device kept a solitary image suspended in the air, but the projector kept the picture flickering at a heightened rate of speed. Though his eyes didn't notice, it prevented the Syndicate cameras from ever getting the comprehensive image.

The photo showed him, standing dressed in his old Vanguard uniform. He was years younger, his eyes were shining a little brighter and his black hair was cut shorter, at regulation length. Dozens of other graduating trainees were in the background, some kissing, some hugging, some posing for other photographers. Then, side-by-side with the younger Clay, stood Jaxon, lean and intense. His tie was a little loose, his uniform a little rough for wear and he was staring down the camera more than anything else.

The picture put a smile on Clay's face.

The alarm blared and, after a moment of hesitation, Clay rolled out of bed. He navigated the dim bedroom with the grace of a nocturnal predator, his feet barely avoiding the various stacks of books and dirty plates dotting the floor. He entered the shower, its frigid water sending chills down his spine. The heater had busted long ago, as far as he could tell. The air conditioning and heating didn't work much better. He'd put through a request for it all to be fixed when he'd moved in, but never really expected anyone to do anything about it. He wasn't an influential member of the Guard and no one expected he'd have much in the way of money. So, there he stood, scrubbing his untamed hair as quickly and efficiently as possible while the icy water sent shivers through every part of his body.

He put his contacts in as he emerged from the icy downpour, then put in his hearlinks. Clay didn't like the Syndicate, but he had to admit they'd outdone themselves with the Creator contacts system.

"Morgan, show me the news," he ordered.

"Yes, sir," the system's AI said, and the lenses came to life. They filled his dim, cheap apartment with vivid color, painting a virtual reality around him. The hearlinks, small though they were, blocked out the whizzing sounds of skycars and distant sirens, replacing them with the Syndicate news channel's starting jingle. Soon enough, it was as if he stood in the midst of a filming studio, the fancy furniture and warm colors surrounding him. The two anchors sat at a glossy table just in front of him, dressed in the monochrome, androgynous clothes that were so popular among the city's wealthier class.

"Show me what you've got," Clay said, starting the program.

"Good morning, and welcome to the Seattle City News," the woman said with a smile. "I'm Clarice Carter-Jones."

"And I'm Jacob Welmer," the man chimed in, sporting an even larger grin. "The war for Central Africa rages as native populations continue to side with dangerous renegade scientist Urias Graff, hindering Syndicate forces in the region from being able to focus on the eradication of infected populations."

Clay put on his clothes and got ready for the day as they spoke. He wore his usual outfit for work: a black t-shirt, denim-polyester jeans, and a pair of black work boots. He grabbed his Orwell handgun from under his mattress as one anchor chimed in, mentioning theories about Graff being a carrier of the CDT virus due to overexposure and experimentation.

Smart move, Clay thought. *Anyone stands up to them, Syndicate scientists call them a carrier or a bug and everyone stops listening.*

"The White Hart promises his army will end this war and begin the process of recolonizing the world outside of currently-approved cities as soon as possible," one of the anchorwomen said. "In spite of the Vanguard's mistakes and the virus' tenacity, the Hart promises Syndicate governors humanity's resurgence within the coming fifty years."

"Of course, he does," Clay said.

"In other news, Chancellor Roy McGrath continues his tour of North America." An image of the Chancellor appeared behind Jacob Miller as he spoke. The large, muscular man stood, adorned in a Black Class Harness, his helmet tucked under his arm. The armor glowed, red, yellow and blue light radiating from the crevices between the black armor plating. McGrath sported a wide, confident grin, and Clay thought he saw a mischievous glint in his eye.

Murderer, Clay thought.

"The Chancellor continues to do regular checks on North American quarantine zones to ensure each is maintaining high-level security and watching over the population's safety."

"Of course, he does," Clay muttered. "End program."

The virtual reality disintegrated around him as he shut the news off, disappearing into his apartment like effervescent, multicolored sand. He stood in the midst of the dim lighting of his room for a moment and took a deep breath.

Focus, man, Clay thought. *One thing at a time. Just get through the day.*

First, he smashed the small hologram under his bed's leg. *I'll get another one from the others*, he thought. The thing would be a liability to carry around all day. He then put on his official City Guard armored jacket, stuffed his notebook into the coat pocket, and approached the small window by his front door.

He peeked through the window, scanning nearby windows and rooftops for any assassins.

The street outside was practically empty, illuminated by the city's fluorescent lighting. Seattle, like all Syndicate cities, was contained within what was, effectively, a miles-wide skyscraper. Skycars flew above Clay, weaving between the buildings built within the city's confines, most of them either freighters or some other type of work vehicle. Few people left their homes unless they absolutely had to, instead choosing to create and explore fantastic worlds with their Creator contacts.

Smart move by the Syndicate. Instead of making the world a better place, give everyone the means to make their own for free, Clay thought. He exited his apartment complex and walked toward the complex's landing pad, watching for anything suspicious or dangerous-looking. In his experience, the city wasn't a safe place.

In Seattle, the majority of those who spent their time in the real world were generally opportunistic criminals who took advantage of the distracted population. He ran into a few of them as he walked through the mess of concrete that composed Seattle's Lower Levels.

Clay walked by a small, skinny man who was pressed, suspiciously, against a nearby apartment door. "What're you doing, Skeez?"

"Moore!" the small, baby-faced thief cried out in surprise. He quickly stepped away from the door. "Headed to work?"

Clay caught a strong whiff of the man's scent. The sickly-sweet smell of oranges clung to his clothes and rode on his breath. "You've got Colombo's scent on you, Donald. You been hitting the club again, smoking that guy's stuff? Maybe need a little more cash to afford another e-cig?"

Donald, who preferred to be called by his thief name, sighed. "Yeah, yeah, I relapsed, but I'm not here to take money, Moore, I swear. I just need some food. You know the Kelsons are in the middle of their morning contact session right now. No fuss, no muss, just a little bit of grub."

Clay nodded, removing his apartment key from his key ring. He tossed it to the skinny, malnourished criminal, who jumped in surprise. "I'm moving out," Clay said. "Help yourself to the stuff in my fridge. I won't be needing it."

"Are you serious?" the lanky fool said shakily. "I couldn't take your food, Moore. We're buddies!" Clay didn't have to be close to Skeez to see the hunger in his eyes betraying the words that came from his mouth.

"Knock yourself out," Clay said as he walked away. "Just get off the vape and quit breaking into people's apartments. You're gonna get yourself killed one day."

The Lower Levels were a filthy, yet awe-inspiring place. The towers, skybridges, and landing pads of the city composed a massive, interweaving network of concrete and steel that sometimes looked like an absolute mess and at other times looked like some abstract monochrome masterpiece. The sky was blocked from sight, the whole city existing within the confines of a massive, concrete skyscraper to keep the Syndicate's 'treasured citizens' from the dangerous 'carriers' outside. Clay passed a sign as he walked, the glowing image mounted to a wall near the local skyship parking range. It showed a nearly porcelain-white man with eyes glowing an ethereal blue. He was holding a truck over his head, an animalistic grimace on his face, teeth bared.

CARRIERS, the sign said. THEY'LL KILL YOU. REPORT A SIGHTING TO YOUR LOCAL CITY GUARD PRECINCT.

If only they knew, Clay thought. He'd recognized the man the first time he'd seen the sign. *No doubt Troy was fighting for his life. Probably got sucked dry by the butchers.*

He sighed, turning away from the poster, and walked on.

One of the local homeless citizens, an old lady covered in a hodgepodge mountain of found overcoats, appeared from a nearby alleyway. She was either very tired or very drunk. "Morning Wendy, how're you doing?" Clay said as he passed by.

Wendy, kind as she was, sweetly cussed him out as he walked away.

"Yeah, you're pretty great, too," Clay said as he mounted his hoverbike.

The small machine hummed as he scanned his thumbprint on the display mounted between the handlebars, the bike's hoverdrive coming to life. Metal clamps secured his legs as a steel support system ran its way up his back and formed a helmet around his head, securing his neck and spine to make sure he wouldn't get any whiplash while flying. Once everything was loaded and in its place, he took off like a rocket into the sky.

The air above the public parking pad was filled, bustling with various schools of skyships, some small, some large. Most of them

5

were cargo ships, entering the city from one of the other North American quarantine zones, but some were taxis and others were personal skyships, though few people had the money to afford such things. Clay zipped between the floating vehicles, his black bike sticking out among the beaten, dull colors of the battered ships surrounding him.

He leaned left, directing his hoverbike into a dive as he turned. He smiled a little, his stomach doing a tap dance as he cut through the sky. He plunged between the various concrete towers of the city, pulling up a few hundred feet above the street below.

He had a few stops to make before he went to the station today, first of which was Mrs. Walker's place. The old widow's home was filled to the brim with kids, most of them covered in filth.

"How're you doing, sweetie?" the woman asked as she opened her door. She still wasn't aware of Clay's name, which was one of the only reasons he was comfortable coming by her home before he went into the station. After he'd done his job, Ice would wipe any record of him from Syndicate surveillance, leaving only a vague memory of "the nice guard" in the old woman's mind and in the minds of her neighbors.

"Just coming by to drop off the usual things," Clay said. He pulled a few bags of groceries from his bike's storage compartment. He'd gone and spent the last of his money on the food last night, just for this occasion. The old lady peeked into them, prodding their bulging contents with her cane.

"More instant soup?" she asked, grateful. "You spoil us all, sir!"

Clay's smile turned genuine as he watched the old woman's face light up. "Well, I can't have a young woman such as yourself going hungry, ma'am," he said.

The old lady giggled. "You're a good man, Mister Guardsman." She led him through the maze of mess and children until they arrived at the equally-chaotic kitchen. "There aren't many people like you anymore."

"You're right on that one," Clay said. "I am, quite literally, one in a million."

The old lady grinned, not understanding the somber meaning of Clay's joke. "Well, I'm glad you know it, at least," she said as she watched the kids sprint around her living room in disorderly, haphazard patterns.

"How're they doing?" Clay asked.

"Oh, they're trouble. As always," the woman said, her voice growing a bit steely. "Either off learning things they shouldn't from the punks on the street or stealing someone's Creator contacts. They'll get themselves killed one day."

"Hopefully not too soon," Clay said.

The old lady shrugged. "At least they'll have fun until then."

That's probably more than I could say, he thought.

"I should probably get going, ma'am, I've got work to do at the station."

"Well, you stay good, young man," the old woman said, leading him back through the swarming kids to the door.

"I'll do my best," Clay promised as they reached the door. Then he was outside, only accompanied by his hoverbike. He sighed. "I promise I'll do my best," he said to no one in particular before mounting the bike and taking off into the sky.

He flew only a short distance, cruising into the Club District. The city's artificial sunlight faded as he entered the area. The club owners had petitioned some time ago to push for dimming the lights in their part of the city. With the sun blocked out by the skyscraper-city's walls, the decision left a whole portion of the Lower Levels stuck in a perpetual night, illuminated only by the light-up signs advertising women, men, drugs, and other such vices.

He landed at a parking pad around the corner of one of the dumpier-looking dives, leaving his Guard's coat inside the bike's storage compartment. He hoped to get things done without too much of a fuss. A sign marked the place as The Hunter's Den, though the *e* and the *n* in Den no longer lit up like they were supposed to. He'd never been to the place before, but it was infamous for being the hangout of Lamar Delacroix, the head of the Lower Club Kings. It was also the favored bar of Dale Barringer, Chief of the 52nd Precinct of the Seattle City Guard and Clay's boss.

This has been a long time coming, Dale, he thought.

However, a bouncer saw him coming and raised his hand to halt Clay long before he'd approached the doors. A few people waiting to enter the run-down bar glanced nervously about, one or two ditching their illicit smoking appliances in the process.

"You need a warrant to enter these premises."

"What if I'm here for the drinks?"

The bouncer frowned.

"What? A man like me can't want a beer?"

"Go get your warrant, Moore."

"How do you know my name?"

"I've been told to watch out for you. A patron of ours says you're something of a dangerous man."

Clay nodded. *Barringer.*

"Come back with a warrant, or don't come back. Understood?"

Clay smiled. "Of course." Then, he pistol-whipped the bouncer up the side of his head. The bouncer, to his credit, kept his legs steady and raised both fists, though the big man's eyes went wide and his jaw went a little slack. Some of the club customers screamed, but Clay didn't pay much mind. He hit the man again, hard, and the bouncer fell, blinking back unconsciousness. Clay was in the door before anyone else could do a thing.

A thick wall of different scents hit his nose, ranging from those imitating the sweet, strong scents of fruit to those simulating the scent of mahogany and high-end leather. The music blared, the bass sending tremors through Clay's chest. The room was dark, lit only by a flashing, colorful lightshow that blinked and spun in time with the music and a dull light over the bar. Bodies were packed into the place, the bar's customers thrashing and thronging in time to the thudding music.

Clay pushed through the crowd to the bar and approached the young bartender, a particularly tough-looking child no older than twelve. "Barringer here?"

The kid frowned and squinted at Clay, shaking up some cocktail.

"Is Barringer here?" Clay said a little louder.

The kid poured the drink and served it to a woman who promptly vanished into the crowded masses.

Clay sighed, putting a few bills on the bar.

The kid's eyes rolled at the meager offering.

Clay put his wallet on the bar.

The kid pocketed the two-fold wallet, then nodded to a hallway at the back of the bar.

"Thanks," Clay yelled over the music before pushing his way through the crowd to the hallway. One or two desperate, hopeful souls pressed their bodies against him, maybe seeking attention. He gave them a polite smile, firmly removed them from his person, and pressed on to the hallway ahead. People here this early in the day were professionals of one kind or another. Professional dancers, professional lovers, and others who professionally sold and provided things keeping the dancers and lovers going. Others were there simply because they could not stand to be anywhere else. They craved the highs of the party, some drug-induced, some sober. These individuals lacked the discipline to refuse it, or they told themselves they did. They either danced with exaggerated motions and starving eyes or they hung around the edges of the room, taking a long drag from their drug of choice. Or, if they were really broke, they snorted a rail of stuff with the texture of sand that some jank had cooked up in a bathroom.

Clay pushed on through them, reaching the hall. The things they offered were cheap bandages. Suppressing emotions and living out a high would not fix the world.

Sure enough, there was a metal door at the end of the hallway. Clay approached it, the light growing dimmer and dimmer the further he went. He reached for the door's handle before realizing there was a thumb-scanner attached.

Don't want visitors, Dale? Clay thought, taking a step back. Concentrating, he summoned his obsidian.

Black material coalesced out of the air, adhering to his body and forming a thick, crystalline shell. Back in the day, the Vanguard's scientists had tried to figure the stuff out. It was definitely some type of carbon-based material, but they'd never been sure how he made it appear and why it did what it did. As it coated his legs, Clay didn't care. He could kick in steel doors and hit really hard. That's what mattered.

He lifted his foot and kicked the door in, frame and all.

A few dancers screamed as he entered, the obsidian spreading to cover the rest of him as he walked. There were a few people Clay recognized seated on a circular couch in the center of the room, most of whom yelped when the door flew off of the wall. Lamar Delacroix was present, as was his cousin and a few of his other lieutenants. Thankfully, not too many members of their gang were there. They all sat, stupefied, watching him enter the room. Some were rigid as stalks, as if they thought he'd stay away from them if they didn't move. A fair number of them stood, guns drawn.

Clay stood, arms extended. "You can take your best shot, boys."

The thugs glanced between themselves until one of the smaller ones pulled a trigger. The bullet hit Clay's shoulder before deflecting into the ceiling. He heard screams out in the main area of the club, though the music kept playing.

Nice part of how shady this place is, Clay thought. *No one gets too surprised by the first few gunshots.*

He drew his own pistol and aimed at the poor gangster. The small man's eyes went wide.

"I'd recommend you drop your weapon, sir," Clay said.

The man obliged.

Clay looked over rest of them, gun in hand. "I'd recommend the rest of you follow suit."

The other guards and gangsters slowly set their firearms on the ground. Clay smiled behind his mask of obsidian, his breath fogging its shiny surface a little.

"Thank you."

The lieutenants and street soldiers nodded anxiously.

As much as Clay enjoyed their worried expressions, they weren't his reason for coming. With all eyes on him, Clay focused in on the man sitting in the midst of them, an oversized E-cig in one hand and a glass of whiskey in the other.

"Morning, Barringer."

One of the men in the room leapt to his feet after Clay spoke. Clay closed the distance in an instant and put the man on his back before he took a second step.

"Another stunt like that, and I infect every last one of you," Clay said. It was a lie, of course. He couldn't infect any of them. As best he knew, no Vanguardsman could. But, that's not what the Syndicate told everybody.

The only benefit I get from being their patsy, he thought.

To his credit, Dale Barringer did his best not to balk at the sight of Clay as his compatriots did. He sat and watched the obsidian fade away from Clay's face, disintegrating into the air. The only sign of fear was the glimmer in his eyes, telling Clay he was screaming on the inside.

"What kind of freak show are you putting on, Moore?" he said. As usual, trying to take control of the conversation.

"The one that ends with you in quarantine for life, *sir*." He emphasized the overly-formal term Barringer had always insisted he use. "That, or permanent expulsion from Syndicate cities. I'm not picky."

Dale did his best smile while Delacroix and the others glanced between him and Clay. "Really. And you think you can just walk out of here afterward, go back to the way your life's been?"

"No, sir. But I don't want to go back to the way my life's been." He shrugged. "Who would? For whatever reason, the different crime families in this city keep sending hit men my way."

Barringer gulped, and Clay saw guilt and fear in the movement, an admission of fault incarnate. But he didn't want a nervous tick, he wanted a verbal confession.

He summoned his obsidian again, willing it to re-cover his face. The dim light of the room made the armor glow and shine. Clay liked it.

"This city's going to know what I am, and when it does, you and the whole 52nd will be quarantined or expelled."

"We're aware that you're a nutcase, Moore. 'Revealing' that won't change anything." Dale's smile was as weak as the pathetic attempt at humor.

He's just burying himself, Clay thought. *Too proud not to go down with the ship.*

He took a step toward the chief of his precinct, some of the assembled gang members and entertainers shrinking away from him in the process. All of them stared, unmoving, riveted at the sight of him. "You don't want to know how I got through the tests, Barringer? All of the background checks and medical exams? Or do you already know?"

He took another step toward the chief. Barringer pulled his gun and fired before Clay got to him, the bullet ricocheting off the obsidian and into one of the walls behind him.

The sound of the gunshot punched through the overwhelmingly loud music emanating from down the hallway. Clay heard some screams and the sound of people running for the exits. A few of the gangsters and dancers in their small room took the opportunity to dart out the door as well.

Clay ignored them, choosing instead to crush the gun's chamber before another shot could be fired. Barringer kept a tough face up, but Clay could see the fear in the man's eyes, the worry as he calculated what this moment meant.

"What do you want?" Barringer asked.

"I want the world to be a better place."

The chaos in the club was louder now. No doubt the dancers had told people he was there. People started to worry, wondering if he'd touched them, but that couldn't be avoided. He consoled himself with the knowledge that the club would be shut down soon enough.

"If you want the world to be a better place, remove yourself from it," Barringer said. "We'd all be grateful."

Clay laughed, but it was an unhappy sound. Rather, it was a frustrated, angry thing. Clay walked over and picked up the damaged door, ramming it back into its place on the wall.

No interruptions.

"I don't think you understand what I'm saying, Dale. I'm saying I want the world to be a better place. I want it to be a place where people like you don't have power. A place where good people can live happy lives."

Barringer stared up at him silently. Everyone who'd been in the room had left already, likely fleeing the scene. The dancers were probably crying, their records possibly being taken by some poor guardsman. The gangsters had places to hide, panic rooms and safe houses to run to. Clay hoped they wouldn't do anything too stupid. As awful as Delacroix was, he helped keep the Lower Levels' criminal underworld in a relative stasis. If he died or got quarantined, there'd be a power vacuum and all sorts of problems came with that.

"So," Barringer said. "What do you want me to do? I can't fix the world."

"You're right, Dale, you can't. So, here's what I want you to do instead." Clay leaned in, until the obsidian shell covering his face was inches from the chief's, fogging a little with the heavy-set man's breath. "I want you to give me your contacts and hearlinks."

The chief obliged, and Clay crushed them.

"Thanks. You won't be calling anyone too soon after this talk of ours. I've got work to do," Clay said. "Now, I want you to say what I am, and I want you to tell me how many of the assassination attempts were coordinated by you."

"Moore…"

Clay raised a finger, holding it one inch from the man's nose. "The Syndicate says I can turn you with one touch, Barringer. One touch and you turn to a bug. Answer the questions."

The chief set his jaw and, for what it was worth, composed himself. "You're a carrier. And I was behind all of them, freak."

Clay tapped the chief on the nose. Barringer took a deep breath, his teeth ground into a snarl. A few tears ran down his face as his mask, the control he'd always cultivated, shattered. Clay could imagine what he was thinking about. He'd seen the vids of transformations as well.

"You answered the question wrong," Clay said. "I'm not a carrier. I'm a Vanguardsman. And that tap is payback."

He punched Dale square in the nose, the obsidian-fueled blow shattering cartilage and knocking him unconscious. Clay punched his way through the club's rear wall and left down an alleyway, obsidian dissipating as he went.

Hopefully he doesn't get too much brain damage from that, he thought. *Want him wide awake when they throw him out of the city.*

2

The City Guard's 52nd Precinct Station was one of the most impressive buildings throughout the Lower Levels despite its size. The place had been built when the quarantine zone was originally established, making it one of the older, smaller buildings in the city. It stood in the midst of the city's grayed towers, its glossy, black walls reflecting the unnatural neon and LED lights from the street. The Syndicate's insignia shone brightly from its position above the main entrance: a shield with the head of a white stag in the center of it.

The station was built during the height of humanity's fight against the infected, back when waves of bugs assaulted cities every day. Though it was shorter than most of the city's buildings, it stood stronger than the rest, its exterior wall crafted to resist high-impact weaponry as well as small-arms fire. Furthermore, City Maintenance made sure it was one of the shiniest buildings in the city, a radiant structure amidst the drab graffiti towers of Seattle's Lower Levels.

Clay sent an audio call to J.J. as he landed on the precinct's parking pad. No risk of anyone else getting suspicious, since no one in the office ever listened to him, anyway.

"Hey man, you good?" J.J. asked. The man sounded tired in spite of the odd tone the speakers gave his voice.

"Yeah, I'm walking into the office right now," Clay said. "You okay?"

"I'm fine. Quite a bit of work riding on this, so it's a bit stressful, that's all."

"Makes sense. I'll get the download started in the next few minutes for you. The data transfer's the easy part of this."

"Alright, man."

"Y'all ready?"

"Ice is recalibrating the skyship's lateral thrusters, but I'll get him in here."

"Beautiful. I'll have Jaxon's room number and some floor plans headed your way within the next few minutes."

"Alright, alright. I'm getting a call from the twins. Talk to you in a bit."

The call ended as Clay walked through the office's main entrance, the automatic doors hissing open. He was pretty excited to demolish the place.

The station's interior was nowhere as clean and polished as its exterior. The lobby was filled with the vapor of various E-cigs, making the whole room reek of a confusing mix of scents. Clay had spent far too much time in the office and, over time, he'd become well attuned to the unique scents of each officer and criminal that frequented the place. He inhaled the fumes, checking for any that might cause him trouble.

He didn't catch any foreign smells, which was good. That meant there was no new talent coming in today, no variables to cause trouble for the operation. It also meant he'd probably get to the server without some hired gun trying to kill him.

He did, however, catch the cinnamon scent of a concoction made especially for Paul, a male prostitute he'd arrested last week. *Guess Tomlinson let her boytoy out*, Clay thought. Sure enough, the guard was reclining in one of the booths lining the room, her man sitting on the seat beside her.

To be fair, she wasn't the only one abusing power. He also smelled the lemony vapor of Mel, a local dealer he'd thrown in a cell a month ago. *Keller and Rodriguez shouldn't have let him out*, Clay thought as he exited the room. The vape he must've paid them with is full of narcotics and stimulants. They'll have strokes within a week.

He walked through the halls, most of the guards ignoring him as he went. Few of them actually spent any time in the office, but those who did were far too busy calling their various contacts on the streets. They were solidifying their cuts of the upcoming profits on the "experimental" E-cig mixes being sold and making sure no one was giving any of the pimps under the station's protection any trouble.

I don't know if it's bad that this stuff doesn't faze me anymore, he thought. A year in the Lower Levels changes things, I guess.

Soon enough, after passing through the maze of concrete halls, he reached the server room. Clay swiped his badge against the door's lock, entering the dust-filled room. Lights flipped on as his presence was sensed, filling the crowded confines with flickering, unnatural light. "Vidcall J," Clay said, walking between the small towers of servers. His hearlinks clicked on, dialing as Clay reached one of the server towers toward the back of the room and turned on its interface.

J.J. appeared a little to the right of Clay, who was already logging in. The lenses placed him a few feet away, his hulking, metal armor etched with a few lines of letters and numbers, turning him into some intimidating monument planted firmly in the middle of the forsaken room. The suit encased his body entirely, containing the dangerous amount of power and flame raging within. Though he looked real as day, Clay felt secure in the knowledge that no one could see the guy but him.

"You in?" J.J. asked.

"Yessir. How are the twins?"

"April says they're on their way out of Atlanta. Their sabotage didn't go quite as well as planned. One of the workers in the water plant got caught in the explosion."

Clay scowled. "I never liked that idea."

"Yeah, well, there weren't any better plans and we needed to draw the Syndicate away from the Institution."

"Did it work? Twins got the intel?"

"Yeah, their deal with the guard captain went through fine and we've got chatter on comm channels about Syndicate transports headed toward the city."

Clay nodded. "So Chik's blackout went without too much trouble?"

"She signed in a few minutes ago and said the power's out and it seems like the failsafes are all in effect."

"Seems like?"

"She programmed herself a path out of there and it's possible it may have caused a glitch in the system. Maybe a few people aren't locked down during the blackout, it's fine."

Clay kept typing. Please let them all be locked down.

"She did her best, Clay."

"I know, I know. Just don't want more people dead."

J.J. sighed. "I know you don't. We're doing our best to keep it safe and streamlined. Speaking of which, you send the data yet?"

Clay plugged in the small, homemade broadcaster, a gift from Ice before he'd entered the city all those months ago. He typed in the final password and clicked Send.

"We're getting it!" Ice yelled in the call's background.

"That answer your question?" Clay asked.

"Yeah, it does."

"Fantastic." Clay smiled. "See you soon, man. Maybe we'll actually all live through this, huh?"

"Of course, we will. We'll meet you at the rendezvous point within the hour."

"Yessir," Clay said. "I'll get to work on getting out of Seattle."

Tomlinson chose that exact moment to burst into the room, writhing, tightly intertwined with Paul. She quickly pulled away when she saw Clay, sending Paul stumbling into one of the server towers.

"What're you doing in here, Moore?" she asked in the most professional voice possible while she cleaned her hair up in order to appear presentable.

"Saving a friend." He tapped his hearlink, ending his call with J.J. A rush of energy ran through his body as black, crystalline armor generated out of thin air, coating his skin and clothes. Shock sprung onto Tomlinson's face and a curse leapt from her lips as Paul shrank back in horror, fear burning in his eyes.

Clay gently slapped them both upside the head, knocking them unconscious, but caught them before they hit the ground. Hopefully, they'd still be able to read and function properly upon waking. He emerged from the server room obsidian-free a few moments later, after cuffing Tomlinson and Paul to a column in the back of the server room. He bent the door's handle at an odd angle, preventing it from easily being opened anytime soon.

He walked through the station with unusual speed, his steps propelled by purpose. He reached the armory in moments. "Can I help you?" the station officer asked. He was also dispatched with a careful slap, though this man went down a bit harder. Clay checked the man's pulse as he hid the large body behind a gun rack. He relaxed a little after feeling the man's heartbeat, confirming he was still alive.

With the guard gone, Clay looted the armory with reckless abandon, equipping himself with some of the higher-grade City Guard battle armor. The obsidian was better, without a doubt, but he could only keep it maintained for so long, so a little extra protection wouldn't hurt. He clipped a dozen concussion grenades into his suit's holsters.

I look like a suicide bomber with all this on, Clay thought as he walked out the armory door. Sure enough, many guards muttered in his wake as he walked through the halls, some making fun, others genuinely concerned. No one acted, however, until Clay reached the lobby.

The guards had taken up formation. Some of them were standing in front of the door, weapons drawn. Others had overturned the booth tables, using them as a cover. The various friends of the guards had all left, leaving the large, circular room silent, wisps of vapor-filled air lingering like ghosts.

I guess Barringer got a hold of some Creator contacts and put a call through, Clay thought.

His obsidian materialized on over his stolen suit of armor just before they opened fire. Useful as the City armor was, he'd rather not have the suit wrecked before he walked out the door. Clay lunged forward, their bullets deflecting off the shining, black surface, ricocheting into a million different directions. Clay moved through them all like a gleaming panther, his crystalline armor reflecting the lobby's dim light in an ethereal manner. Through it all, he stayed focused, concentrating to maintain the obsidian barrier that defended him in spite of the barrage of bullets and blows.

Can't get too carried away, he thought. *They think you're the bad guy. You've got to prove them wrong.*

Still, it was hard not to enjoy himself. *Hi there, Ramirez*, he thought as he dislocated one of the bigger guards' shoulders, *I bet you're regretting trying to rig my bike to blow a few weeks ago.* Another guard fired at him from behind, but her handgun's bullets were less effective than a mosquito bite. She was incapacitated in seconds with a broken wrist and ankle.

Before three minutes had passed, Clay stood alone in the room, haloed by the lobby's dim lights. The guards were all either unconscious, injured, or gone, having fled in fear. Only one guard from the barricade remained untouched. Keller stood in the doorway, his belly bulging out from under his bulletproof vest. He stood, frozen, his eyes wide and glassed over with shock. Clay walked towards the man, easily disarming him.

"Hey Keller," Clay said as he faced the overweight guard, "How's your day going?"

Keller began hyperventilating, his eyes rooted to Clay's as if his intimidating form were magnetic and the guard's eyes were two glossy bolts.

"That's what I thought," Clay said, bending Keller's gun in half. "Where are the others? The whole Assault Division's gone."

The guard was wheezing now.

Clay allowed the armor coating his right hand to dissolve into the air, then slapped the guard with it. The man stopped wheezing, though his eyes still bulged with panic.

"They're at Angel's Landing," Keller said quietly, staring down at his own feet. "We got word from the gangs that they'd found the Angel's hideout. They're gonna go arrest anyone they find."

Clay frowned. "The Angel? They found the Angel?"

Keller nodded.

Clay's frown deepened into a scowl. Just my luck.

"Am I going to die now?" Keller whimpered.

"Not right now," Clay said. "Does it look like I'm here to kill you?"

"No," Keller said pathetically. Tears welled up in his eyes, his voice rising in hysteria. "You're leaving us all to suffer. You're twisted and you're a carrier and you're gonna make us all bugs!"

Clay sighed. "Keller, how long have I been working here?"

The guard's eyebrows knitted together. "I dunno, a few months? A year or two?"

"According to the Sydicate, how long ago should you have been infected?" Clay said.

The guard's brow pressed further in on itself. He obviously wasn't getting the message.

"If the White Hart and his Chancellors were right, you'd have been made a bug the first time you shook hands with me," Clay said. His armor reformed around his bare hand and Keller flinched. "Looks like you can't believe everything you're told."

He broke his panicked colleague's nose, causing him to scream and curl up in a ball. Clay cuffed him for good measure and left.

"Vidcall J," he said, walking to the parking pad. The big man in the metal suit appeared to his right again, floating along with Clay as he walked.

"What's up, Clay? I can't talk long, the others are calling in. We're all starting to converge. Something wrong?"

"Only a little," Clay said.

"Well, be fast about it. What's up?"

"You remember the Angel? The vigilante I told you about?"

"Yeah, your celebrity crush. What about her?"

"Turns out the City Guard's got her. They're at Angel's Landing right now busting into her safehouse."

J.J. took a deep breath.

"I know, I know, we're on a tight schedule," Clay said as he reached the parking pad. "But I can get to her and get out in time! This city needs her, man. She's pushing out the gangs, helping take on the corruption, everything!"

"Clay, no," J.J. said. "We're busting Jaxon out. That's the mission, that's what we agreed on."

"But J, Seattle…"

"Is a city with a massive armory of weapons made to take down people like us and jam-packed with millions of people who've bought into the Syndicate's story" J.J. shook his head. "Get out, man. It isn't safe. We'll be at the pickup point in four hours or so."

The call ended before Clay could say another word. He stood on the parking pad, glancing at the clock on one of the nearby skyships.

You can't, the sensible part of him thought. *You'll get caught or be late. Something will go wrong, you'll make a mess. It's happened before.*

Yeah, it has, and I'm still alive, Clay thought.

By sheer luck and the help of your friends, the sensible part of the mind said. *Are you going to risk breaking Jaxon out for someone you don't know?*

Clay revved his skybike, taking off into the air.

I don't rank people, he thought. *I save them.*

3

Clay was halfway to Angel's Landing when the city's fluorescent lighting turned blood red and began flashing. A warning blared through the city's intercom.

"*Warning*," the computer-generated voice said, roaring through countless speakers. "*A carrier has breached the quarantine zone. Repeat: a carrier has breached the quarantine zone. Theta Protocol is now in effect. Ground all vehicles and prepare for containment.*"

The air of the city reverberated as millions of doors automatically closed and locked themselves, barricading the population into their homes, workplaces, and public spaces while simultaneously blocking the streets into manageable regions.

Keeps them away from me, Clay thought. The cries and screams of the city population could be vaguely heard through the blaring sirens. Clay could imagine them, children crying and mothers panicking as they thought of the horrific carrier, roaming their city like a monstrous predator doing all it could to infect them and transform them into soulless shells like the loved ones they'd lost.

Syndicate's way too good at propaganda, he thought.

He flew through the sky as fast as he could. All the other skycars had landed by now, clearing the airways to avoid him or, more accurately, the monster they thought he was. As convenient as it was for Clay, he knew that it'd benefit the Guard even more.

Sure enough, he saw approaching drones out of the corner of his eye. They were bigger than the usual machines made for surveillance, hovering above and about the large public spaces of Syndicate cities. They swarmed around his skybike like a flock of glossy, black birds.

Clay put the bike into a dive, ramming some of the drones out of his way before the others behind him opened fire. The black, triangular devices in front of him crumbled as the other drones' bullets pierced their aluminum hulls, sending them tumbling haphazardly through the sky. The still-functioning drones dove after Clay, peppering his bike with a few rounds. He summoned his obsidian just in time. A bullet clipped his shoulder, harmlessly ricocheting off into the air.

"Please let this work," Clay muttered as he pulled up and out of his dive, narrowly managing to steer the skybike into a maintenance hole in one of the surrounding towers. The drones did their best to follow him, though most had to rapidly decelerate to do so. Clay twisted and turned his way through the maintenance tube, narrowly avoiding crashing a number of times, the bike's sides grinding against the tube's interior.

He leaned into another wrenching turn and glanced over his shoulder, accidentally scraping the bike's side on the wall as he did so. The drones were gaining on him, steel birds riding on his tail. Their sleeker design and smaller size gave them advantages in such confined spaces.

That dive didn't slow them down as much as I needed it to, he thought.

He pulled out of another turn. He could see red flashing lights ahead, shining through the maintenance shaft exit. He hit the accelerator. The hoverdrive's hum rose an octave as it strained to push him through the sky faster.

"Definitely didn't work," he said to himself as the tumultuous sound of gunfire erupted behind him and a stream of bullets pelleted holes in the back of his skybike. The bike's hoverdrive began to wheeze and sputter.

Peachy, Clay thought. Sparks shot into the air around him, streaming like falling stars. Adrenaline burst through his veins as his skybike began to dive.

It was both a good and bad thing that the bike managed to get out of the maintenance shaft. It was good because he'd have been stuck with no way to get down if the bike had come to a stop in the shaft. The downside was, the only way down now was a crash landing, and a rough one at that.

He braced himself as the bike turned into a nosedive, still spewing sparks. It added its own beeping alarm to the ruckus of the locked-down city as its various crash protocols activated. The falling bike was streaking through the sky, gaining speed as it cruised downward.

Just crash already, Clay thought.

The bike's emergency thrusters kicked on before the collision, trying to pull the bike back upright so it wouldn't hit the ground nose-first. Even still, the vehicle was demolished by the crash landing. The aluminum body of the bike crumbled, its titanium internal framing compressed with the impact as the rear thruster entirely detached. A few pressure redistribution bags deployed where Clay was sitting, trying to cushion his impact as much as possible.

Won't be enough, Clay thought.

He kept his obsidian up, focusing on it as he hit the ground. His crystalline armor cracked ever so slightly, little spider webs of broken material etched into the surface right in front of his eyes. He tore one of his hands from the skybike's safety restraints and pried his other hand out of the wreckage. He watched the sky, eyeing the descending drones, then staggered to his feet and darted toward a nearby alleyway. A few of the drones opened fire, their bullets glancing off his shoulders and back.

Well, this could be going better, Clay thought. *This could be going a lot better.*

4

Dune

If we survive this, Natalie's got to give me a week-long vacation from this insanity, Dune thought.

He glanced at his sister. She sat, dressed in her dented white-and-gold battle armor that had earned her the nickname "Angel." She kept her rifle and scope pointing out one of the holes in the wall, monitoring the street outside. The old place they'd bought years before was about as ragged as their combat gear. Bullet holes dotted the walls and the street outside was marred with residual marks of explosions. They'd known the building would hold longer than most. It was one of the reasons they'd bought it. The one-room home was one of the older constructs in the Lower Levels and could only be approached from two directions, as it was built into one of the outer corners of the city.

Still, won't hold for long, he thought. *Only a matter of time before they get permission to send in the big guns.*

His peripheral vision caught something moving. A City Guard fire team was advancing through one of the nearby buildings. He checked through his rifle's infrared scope, poking the suppressed muzzle over the windowsill.

"Four tangoes approaching from the diner to the north," he said.

"Ground floor?" Natalie asked.

"Yep."

An explosion tore through the diner, decimating the tables and chairs inside. The explosion threw the four guards like they were rag dolls.

"I put a proximity mine in there last week."

"Of course you did."

"You both know you're insane, right?" Sage said. The nurse was lying on the floor, out of the view of any snipers, surrounded by the decimated remains of servers and interfaces. She was operating on herself, a piece of shrapnel having hit her in the leg when she'd tried to leave earlier.

"Shut up," Natalie said. "More are coming."

They sat in silence for a few seconds, Dune crouching behind the wall, watching for more oncoming guards through his scope. He heard three quiet bursts emit from his sister's rifle.

"They're down," she said.

"Seriously insane," Sage repeated.

"Yeah," Dune said. "Probably."

He watched Sage out of the corner of his eye. Her dexterous hands were tying off the stitches she'd given herself, bloody shrapnel on the ground beside her. He shook his head, looking through his rifle's scope again, scanning nearby buildings for movement.

She doesn't deserve any of this mess, he thought.

He felt responsible, of course. He'd been the one to ask the nurse to help them years ago. She was just some lady across the hall from their apartment who helped patch Natalie up. It was supposed to be a one-time thing. He'd acted out of instinct and panic, asking Sage to stitch her up.

Now she's bleeding on the floor, Dune thought.

He spotted two guards setting up a sniper nest in a nearby apartment building. One went down with the first shot. He clipped another, finishing him with a second shot.

"They're about to try something," Dune said.

"Like what?" Sage said. She'd finished tying off her stitches and was putting away the needle and thread.

"Probably hit us with some explosives. Maybe drop some guards on the roof. They're just throwing bodies at us right now, trying to keep us occupied."

"So, what're you going to do?" Sage asked.

Natalie fired off another two rounds. "Open the grate."

"What?" Sage said.

"Open the grate next to you."

Dune watched the street as they bickered. His scope's infrared screen blinked out for a second. He rattled the rifle, banging on the faulty mechanism. They'd taken a hit or two earlier, when the City Guard first fired on the house. He and Natalie were lucky they'd been about to go out on patrol. Dune's blue, now-dented battle armor was the only reason he'd survived the initial attack.

"Teach your sister to defend herself, they said," Dune grumbled under his breath, "She'll be safe that way, they said."

"They were right," Natalie said.

The scope flickered back on in time for Dune to see a particularly large heat signature coming from behind a nearby building. It was a few heads taller than Dune, probably around seven feet, with limbs twice as thick as his.

A Harness, Dune thought. He scowled. Then the thing burst through the concrete wall it'd been hiding behind.

"Get the grate open!" Dune yelled. Two bullets leapt from his rifle, striking the Harness's neck and ricocheting off without leaving a scratch. The silver suit of armor moved like a freight train, slow at first but unstoppably gaining speed. Natalie cursed behind him, likely feeling the thing's steps as it shook the pavement beneath them. Dune fired another round, then another, aiming for a small spot near the armored neck where the optic sensory array was tucked away.

Come on, he thought.

The grate screeched behind him, finally opened.

His next bullet didn't even leave a mark. The Harness was almost on top of him.

Yeah, screw this, Dune thought. He turned to the grate, which was still open like some metal jaw. He caught a glimpse of Natalie climbing down into the sewers below. Her eyes met his before spotting something over his shoulder, going wide at the sight.

That was when he heard the Harness arrive. The armor's collision with the thick, reinforced wall of the building sounded like thunder, or maybe an earthquake, resonating as the broken pieces of concrete tumbled into one another and into the war machine. One head-sized piece of wall caught Dune in the back, sending him tumbling forward. For a moment, everything was directionless, the ground collided with the back of his facemask, then his back. His vision blurred the ground and ceiling into one chaotic blend. Then, the floor went out from under him. He fell, feeling nearly weightless, unable to connect with anything solid until he landed in sewage with a splash.

Guess I made it into the sewers, he thought, sinking through to the filthy tunnel's bottom. Then he thought, *I think I lost my rifle.*

His helmet quickly began filling with putrid fluid. From somewhere far above, a muffled boom managed to reach him through the grime and liquid, shaking his rib cage with its ferocity.

Guess Nat blew the building. Probably not seeing that rifle again.

He resurfaced, pulling his helmet from his head. First, he realized his beard and long, curly brown hair were both soaked in sewer water. Some of it touched his tongue as he took his first breath; if it weren't for the shock and adrenaline, he would've retched. As he looked up, he found their safe house was, indeed, in flames. Some of the water around him was aflame as well, making him wonder what people were flushing down their toilets. The sewer had obviously been in good condition at one point, but had been forsaken, much like the streets and neighborhoods above. The remains of concrete and metal walkways lined the walls, but some had caved in at some point and others had been submerged over time.

Natalie came to the surface a few feet from him, her helmet also missing and her bun of dark brown hair now sopping wet. Her dark eyes were notably more intense in the flames' light.

Her hands flashed a few signals. **Hostile still standing. Follow. Quiet.**

Roger, he signaled back. **I'm unarmed. Where's Sage?**

Near, Natalie signed. **Follow.**

She motioned towards one of the sewer's walls and silently led him to it. There, securely taped high on the wall, was a pistol and a few magazines of ammo.

He shook his head, smiling. *You would,* he thought. She boosted him up and he pulled it all from the wall, making sure to hold the gun and ammunition above the water level. No need for any "foreign objects" to find their way into the barrel or mechanisms.

Follow, Nat signaled once again.

He nodded.

They moved silently for a few moments, Natalie recovering her rifle from a piece of metal walkway she'd left it on and grabbing a backpack that'd been securely taped to the wall at a different point. They heard the Harness moving above, stomping around their former haven. It tore away at the concrete and rebar back near the sewer entrance, likely trying to make the entrance large enough for its considerable girth. Meanwhile, Dune and Natalie half-walked, half-swam deeper into the tunnel to where it intersected with another sewer tunnel, the high levels of the sewage keeping either of them from moving quickly.

"Hey," a voice whispered from the shadows. Dune whirled, nearly shooting the speaker until he realized it was Sage.

"Sorry," she said.

"Shh," Natalie said.

Sage scowled through the painful grimace on her face, presumably caused by her stitched leg.

That won't be good, Dune thought.

They turned right and continued their swim-walking through the sewer. As the adrenaline and shock began to fade, Dune's neck, back, and head started hurting and his mind was beginning to churn. There were only so many exits they could take to get out of this part of the sewer system. All of them would be heavily guarded.

We're walking to our deaths, he thought. Somewhere in the distance, loud alarms were going off. *Siccing the whole city on us? That's a bit much.*

Back around the corner, something crashed into the sewer.

And there's the Harness, he thought. *Beautiful.* He looked to Natalie again.

Follow, she signed.

Well, of course, Dune thought.

He obeyed, but his mind continued to fly as he went. They'd been routed by a Gray Class Harness. It wasn't even a Black Class Harness and they'd been forced out of their position and into a dangerous situation. If they managed to get away from it and elude its friends that were undoubtedly waiting for them at any sewer entrance, it was only a matter of time before they'd be ID'ed by the city's surveillance system and visited by another platoon of guards, with likely even bigger guns ready. Who knew what the city would be like, anyway. The sound of the alarms continued to echo along with them as they walked. On the one hand, it covered their splashing steps. But the blaring sound was a constant reminder of how in it they were now.

We're dead, he thought. He spotted Natalie, trying to figure out how he'd get her out of this one. They'd been through plenty together, but this took the cake.

Nat looked unconcerned, all things considered. She motioned Dune over to one of the sewer walls as they followed the path and came to a point where the roof was especially high. He followed while Sage stayed put, watching out for the prowling Harness. At Natalie's gesturing, Dune boosted her up until she was barely able to reach the ceiling. Then, bracing herself against the sewer wall, she reached into her backpack and pulled out a large explosive charge.

Oh boy, Dune thought. The sloshing sound of something large moving toward them whispered through the sewers behind them. Natalie worked furiously, pulling extra-durability tape she'd retrieved from her bag to tape the explosive to the wall multiple times over.

Down, Natalie signaled, and he lowered her, taking extra care to make sure not to cause unnecessary splashing. She tossed her backpack onto a nearby shelf of concrete, snapping a few times until she eventually got Sage's attention.

"What?" Sage whispered.

"Shhh," Natalie said. Her hands motioned and pointed for a few seconds to no avail. Amidst it all, Dune picked up on one consistent signal: **Hide**.

Sage, having never learned what their signals meant, was endlessly confused.

Natalie scowled. Then, without another word, she submerged herself down into the sewage.

Sage turned to Dune, still unaware of the command. "What did she say?"

"Hide," he whispered. He stuck his pistol on top of the backpack then joined Natalie, curled up in the filthy water. *My beard and hair are gonna be gross again,* he thought, eyes and mouth firmly pressed closed.

For a second or two, there was no sound and Dune was alone with the darkness and the warped sounds one hears when underwater. Every second, something bumped into him. He sincerely hoped it was Natalie or Sage.

The sewer floor shook with a loud, echoing step. Then another, and another, and another. The steps drew closer and grew louder until they were all he heard, all he thought about.

We're blind like this, he thought. *The Harness could be on top of us, for all we know. Hopefully Sage hid. But, who knows, maybe she didn't hide. I can't tell, now.*

Another step.

Maybe she's dead.

Another step. This one shook the sewer floor, rocking Dune as he floated amidst the grime and sludge. He braced himself against the grimy surface of the sewer, his lungs stinging.

Leave already, leave already, leave already.

The Harness didn't take another step. Seconds ticked by. Dune's throat demanded air. His jaw felt as if it had a mind of its own and was determined to open and let the flow of rancid water in at any second.

Yeah, screw it, he thought.

He stood slowly, disgusting water dribbling out of his beard and long, brown hair. There, in front of him, stood the huge, silver Harness, facing him down.

"Good morning," Dune said.

The Harness didn't take the time to be so polite.

The large machine of war grabbed Dune's battle armor by the breastplate, raising him up and out of the sewage. For a second, he just hung there, crap and water dripping off his body, staring into the Harness's metal face. He'd seen very few Harnesses in person before, he's mostly seen the advertisements. THE ONLY REAL PROTECTION IN AN INFECTED WORLD, they had always said.

Pretty ironic at the moment, he thought.

"You have been identified as Douglas Warner."

The statement surprised Dune. He'd expected to be killed, outright. He quickly scanned the sewer, checking for any possible ways out. While he found none, he did see Sage slowly rising. She held in a gag, going wide-eyed.

"Friends call me Dune," Dune said, trying to keep the Harness's attention.

"Well, we're not friends."

"Touché." Dozens of strategies were going through his head. He had to find a way for Sage and Nat to get out. Sage limped away from the Harness slowly, almost silently.

No way the sewage is treating her stitches well, he thought. *Might only be able to get Nat out.*

He steeled himself. He'd had to make harder decisions. He hadn't known Sage all that long. Maybe if he drew the Harness's attention to Sage, Nat would be able to get out.

"You're under arrest, Warner," the Harness said.

"Yeah, I figured."

The Harness held up a pair of reinforced handcuffs, holding them between two massive fingers. "Put these on."

Dune scanned the Harness. "Where'd you pull those from?"

"That doesn't matter." The Harness shoved the cuffs into Dune's chest. "Put them on."

"Okay, okay," Dune said, fumbling with the large, metal restraints. "I was curious." He couldn't think of a better plan. Sage was going to have to take the fall.

"It's a compartment in the leg," said the Harness.

"That's useful."

Dune's lips parted, ready to utter Sage's death sentence, when an

29

odd ringing sound echoed through the sewer.

"What's that?" the Harness said.

"Hell if I know," Dune said. "No one tells me anything around here." *What've you got planned, Nat?*

The Harness turned once or twice, trying to figure out where the sound came from. Sage barely managed to duck in time to avoid being spotted and, for a second, Dune panicked, having lost his only possible opportunity to save Nat. Then, once the Harness was done turning about, she resurfaced and Dune relaxed a little.

The ringing was barely louder than the echoing alarms. One of the armor's huge, silver fingers pointed at Nat's backpack.

"What's in there?"

"I don't know."

"Of course not," the Harness chuckled.

Dune's eyebrows rose. *That's a sound I never expected to hear.* Before he knew what was happening, he was back in the sewage.

He came up spluttering, wiping all sorts of garbage and excretion from his face and armor. He stood in the midst of a semi-solid mound that must have formed within the sewer over time.

Douche dropped me in a literal island of crap, Dune thought.

"Pick up the backpack, Warner."

Dune stumbled through the disgusting island. He was too busy spitting, coughing, and hacking to respond with any witty retort. His mouth had a moist, sandy texture that nearly made him vomit every time he thought about it.

I'd better not get some nasty bug from this, he thought. *Been through too much to die from a disease I got from some guy's flushed piss.*

Though the filth kept him from speaking, he was still able to do a quick scan of the sewer as he stood and grabbed the backpack. Sage was still limping away quietly, a little ways behind the Harness. She winced with each step.

Tough lady, Dune thought. But his attention was more drawn to something behind the Harness.

There, rising from the urine and garbage, was Natalie. She'd lost her helmet, too, and her near-black hair was as soaked as his. Her face was smeared with something particularly unpleasant-looking. In general, she looked like something that belonged in a sewer.

Hope I don't look like that, Dune thought.

"Quit stalling, Douglas," the Harness said.

Out of the corner of his eye, he watched Natalie sign something, but couldn't tell what it was. *Can't look at you right now, Nat, unless you want the big robo-armor catching sight of you.*

"Open the bag."

Natalie nodded. Twice. That, he could see.

He opened the bag slowly, and was surprised to find only the detonator for the explosive Nat had likely taped somewhere and a small, silver rectangle. It had an illuminated flat screen and was beeping obnoxiously.

Wait, Dune thought. *I've heard of these.* He held it up to the Harnessed soldier.

"What is it?" the Harness said.

"I believe it's called a phone. Basically, it's a super old comms device." He stared at the screen. It said Clive in big, white letters.

Oh, God is good.

"Answer it."

Dune nodded. "Yes, sir. Or ma'am. I don't know who's in there, and I certainly don't want to assume."

"Just answer it."

Dune clicked the green button on the screen and held the old gadget to his ear.

"Natalie, you there?" The old man's smooth voice had never been so welcome in Dune's ears.

"It's Dune." He scanned the area as he spoke, searching for the explosive the trigger in the bag would set off.

"Well, hello, Douglas! You've never used my gadgets before. I'm so proud."

"Make it louder," the guard in the Harness ordered.

Dune shrugged. "Doesn't work that way," he lied. He said back to the phone, "What do you want?"

"No need to be so harsh, Douglas. I was calling to discern your location. Now that I've got it, I'll be there in a few."

Dune's eyes spotted a faint, blinking light on the ceiling as Clive spoke. Sure enough, there were the charges, stuck to the sewer ceiling.

Beautiful, Dune thought, positioning the Harness between the explosive and himself.

"Don't move," the Harness said.

"Shhh," Dune said, gesturing at the phone.

The Harness growled.

"Sorry, I was just talking to someone," Dune said into the phone. "Oh yeah? Screw you, too!" He glanced at the Harness, hoping the soldier inside the suit of armor was buying the act.

"Douglas, we'll need to talk about manners later," Clive said on the other line. "Nonetheless, I'll see you shortly."

With that, the phone shut off.

"Who was it?" the Harness said.

"I don't know. Some guy. He was pretty rude."

"Sure."

Dune heard commotion further down the sewer. He turned, hopeful, until he saw the gray armor of average City Guard grunts. They were wrangling Sage, wrestling her in the filth.

So, selling her out is no longer an option, he thought.

The Harness saw them too, then turned to Dune. "Friend of yours?"

Dune shrugged. "Don't know her." He did his best to say it quiet enough to keep Sage from hearing. From her betrayed expression, he guessed he'd failed. A few of the guards began wading their way over to him. He glanced back where Nat had been a second or two ago. She was gone.

Good.

The Harness turned. "What're you looking at?"

"Nothing, sorry. Zoned out. Thinking about impending death and everything."

"Dune!" Sage screamed. They were starting to drag her away now. "Dune!"

He didn't look at her.

"Thought you said your friends call you Dune?"

"What can I say? Common name."

"No, it isn't."

Dune shrugged.

Some automatons, City Guard-issue, popped out of an opening further down the sewer, marching like an army of mannequins. They were standard Syndicate models with pill-shaped heads, a coat of black paint, and a shield with the head of a white stag in the center of it adorning their chests. Only one guardsman was at all concerned about them.

"Anyone call in the stickmen?" he asked.

That was when the automatons opened fire.

Bullets struck like scalpels, dropping the guards surrounding Sage in one volley. The guards approaching Dune reached for their weapons but absorbed their own volley before they could draw a single weapon.

The Harness watched Dune, who was smiling through his filthy beard, detonator in hand.

"Tables turn, officer."

He pulled the trigger before the Harness could stop him.

The explosion rocked the sewer, blowing the roof off of the place and knocking the Harness a few steps forward. Dune hunkered down, using the Harness's big frame to shield himself. The big guy threw a punch and Dune dodged to the side, submerging, once more, into the sewage, which was now aflame in some areas. He swam low, bumping into the disgusting sewer floor a few times, sludge and water muffling the sound of gunshots. A piece of falling debris hit him, knocking his face into the floor beneath. He kept swimming, blind and breathless, until two hands grabbed him by the legs, strong as clamps.

Lots of being lifted and dropped today, he thought.

His kicking and struggling didn't relieve him from the grip. If anything, the hands held tighter and pulled harder. Two more grabbed him by his armor's belt. Then, spluttering, he was back above water.

"You ought to relax a little, Douglas." The yell managed to overpower the sound of the continued gunshots and chaos. Dune recognized the voice immediately. He breathed deep and took a moment, wiping down his face with as much poise as he could muster while hanging upside down. He opened his eyes with the most neutral half-smile he could muster.

"Morning, Clive. Could you have your stickmen turn me right-side up, please?"

The older man stood in front of Dune, two other automatons holding a small platform for him to stand on, keeping it a foot or two above the sewage. As usual, the hacker was dressed in a pristine charcoal suit with a white shirt and a bright-green tie. Immaculately polished leather shoes rounded out the ensemble.

"Good morning to you too," Clive said, flashing a bleach-white smile. "I suppose I could have them help you stand, but I like to leave people hanging."

"That checks out. Didn't think you were the type to visit these kinds of people. The smell doesn't match your cologne too well."

"Oh, don't worry about me. I'll burn this suit. I've literally got a closet full of them." He held a controller of sorts in his hands, one that looked like it belonged to some kid's game. Nevertheless, the automatons moved as he pressed and clicked.

Guess that's what matters, Dune thought. "What's happening?" he yelled. As far as he could hear, a battle was happening a few feet behind him.

"Oh," Clive said, "right." With a quick button click, the automatons holding Dune began turning about. "There, now you've got a view."

The Harness was lashing out like a cornered bear, surrounded by a small brigade of automatons. They moved and interacted with one another nearly fluidly, no doubt aided by their adaptive strategy programming. Natalie, as insane as always, was right there with them, gun in hand.

She will be the death of me.

Another automaton separated itself from the insanity, cradling a wincing, filthy Sage.

"Why are the city automatons helping us?" she yelled.

"Because I told them to, ma'am," Clive said with a smile. "Clive de Santos. Charmed, I'm sure."

Sage looked to Dune, completely in the dark. Dune gave his best upside-down shrug.

"He's a hacker," Dune said.

"And an informant," Clive amended. "And a general connoisseur of life."

"Sure," Dune said, "that too." He was too busy analyzing the conflict to care about Clive's gloating. The automatons' guns hit harder than the standard Syndicate rifles, but the Harness's armor was holding. Sure, it was dented and scratched where the bots had focused fire, but it was still functioning fine. Meanwhile, the Harness couldn't get a hand on the stickmen. They'd lost one or two early on, but the others had adapted. They anticipated punches and scattered whenever the thing lunged at them. Natalie had retreated, thank goodness, but only far enough to be out of the Harness's reach. She continued to fire on the thing, though her bullets did less than the automatons'.

It's a stalemate, Dune thought. *We can't afford a stalemate. The big guy will get reinforcements and no one's coming to back us up.*

He looked to Clive. "We gotta pull back."

"Seems that way, doesn't it?"

"Can we, please?" Sage said. "I need to disinfect my leg."

"Nat!" Dune yelled. "We're leaving!"

"Give me a second!"

Dune turned to Clive again. "Have one of the automatons bring her. She's not gonna listen."

Clive's brows raised, eyes never leaving the battle before them. "Are you sure that'd be a good idea, Douglas? She may not take well to being forced."

"I don't take well to dying from an infection!" Sage yelled. "Let's go!"

One of the automatons separated from the others and marched

toward Natalie. She put a bullet in its head.

"Told you she wouldn't take to it well," Clive said.

Dune scowled. *Gotta do it all myself.*

Before he could take a single step forward, the Harness lunged. The automatons automatically parted, easily dodging the anticipated attack. Natalie, however, was not as quick. The Harness loomed to its full height, its large, metal hand firmly gripping Natalie by the collar.

"Everybody back," the Harness said. It held Nat like a piñata, though this particular piñata was determined to continue hitting back, shooting her pistol's few remaining rounds into the Harness. Then she threw the pistol.

Dune rolled his eyes. *Death by pride.*

With a casual flicking of two clasps, Natalie detached the lower half of her body armor from the upper half and dropped, gracefully, back into the sewage, immediately disappearing into the muck.

For a moment, everyone stood silently, the sound of alarms echoing through the sewers and blaring in their ears. After a second of hesitation, the Harness's pilot dug its massive hands through the surrounding rancid water, searching for its elusive prey. One or two of the automatons, meanwhile, reloaded their firearms as quietly and discreetly as possible.

"Can we go, now?" Sage said.

Before another word was said, a soldier covered in black, glossy armor fell through the hole Nat's bomb had created in the sewer's roof. The soldier landed on top of the much-larger Harness, pushing it down into the sewage. The huge splash splattered yet another layer of filth onto Dune's soiled face.

"My suit!" Clive yelled.

The man in black ignored him.

A Vanguardsman, Dune thought. *That's a twist* . He hadn't seen one with this particular ability before, but there was no mistaking the guy.

One crystalline fist struck the Harness in the chest, propelling the large, metal suit of armor a few feet back and sending a decent wave through the sewer. The Vanguardsman pressed the advantage, bridging the gap with a lunge and delivering a solid kick to the armor's chest. The Harness lost its footing entirely, this time falling flat on its back into the sewage. It tried to stand, but the newcomer was already on top of it, dealing blow after blow to the Harness's breastplate, repeatedly pushing it further into the muck. Dune watched as the previously impenetrable silver armor steadily crumbled before him, unimpressed. He glanced at the others. Sage watched with a blend of shock and fear in her eyes while Clive looked on with a wide smile, giddy as a fat kid in a burger joint. Natalie, too, resurfaced and watched ravenously.

Dune frowned. *She'll bring this up later.*

The man in black crystal reached his fingers into the newly-made gap between the Harness's central plating, the metal screeching as it bent. He delivered a quick punch and the Harness went still.

"You kill 'em?" Dune asked.

"Just knocked them unconscious." The Vanguardsman hoisted the much-larger Harness over his head, leaning the immobile armor against the sewer wall, making sure the head stayed above water.

Noble, too, Dune thought. *He is trouble.*

The Vanguardsman turned to face them, all armor but his leg gear melting away like trippy ash. That stuff kept the sewage off, no doubt.

And he's ruggedly handsome, Dune thought.

"Which one of you is the Angel?" the man asked.

Natalie raised her crap-soaked hand.

The man smiled a little. "Impressive! You're younger than I thought you'd be."

Natalie blushed. "I'm nineteen?"

"Well, you're doing pretty well, I think," the man said.

Dude, you don't even know, Dune thought. He caught Sage glancing about at everyone while they stood. Clive, meanwhile, still stood with a wide smile, absentmindedly wiping dung from his suit.

"Well," the Vanguardsman continued, "thanks for not screaming at the sight of me. I've got to go, but I'll keep their attention on me as best I can, try and keep the heat off of you." He turned away, his armor reforming in an instant. His voice was muffled with the facemask on, but Dune was pretty sure the guy said, "Live a good life and all that," before he leapt back out of the hole in the sewer's ceiling.

They stood in silence for a second, the blaring alarms echoing through the sewers.

"Well," Sage said. "Can we please, please leave?"

Dune nodded, and they left.

5

Clive still had that ridiculous smile stuck to his face.

Dune sat in one of the nice, well-stuffed couches of the informant's safe house, a can of beer in his hand and a few Koolpacks taped to his chest and back. The icy, sharp touch numbed his throbbing bones as he scrubbed his hair with a silky, soft towel. He'd washed himself around three times over, washed his mouth out at least as many times, but the smell and unbearable taste lingered a little.

Least my hair feels nice, he thought. It'd been a while since he'd gotten to blow dry it.

The apartment was nicer than most of the safe houses Dune had been to before. It was a more secluded place, perched on the outer ring of Seattle's Upper Levels. The view was positively stunning. All exterior walls were Smart-tint windows, which let him look out into the dark, star-filled night outside the city without letting anyone see inside. In the distance, a golden sun rose over the suburb ruins of Old Seattle.

Been years since I saw one of those, he thought as he gazed at the golden horizon. *It looks about the same as I remember.*

Clive reentered the room, having ended a hearlink conversation. "We'll be smuggled on a freighter leaving at six o'clock tonight," the man said cheerily, his gray hair newly washed and his bristling beard just trimmed. He also donned a new, powder-gray suit, the old one having been disposed of the moment they returned. He glanced at the two empty beer cans Dune had left on the glossy kitchen countertop.

"Help yourself," he said. "I'm more of a wine drinker. What do you think of the place?"

"What's with the tree?" Dune asked.

Clive laughed wholeheartedly, turning to face the alien-like organism sprouting out the center of his apartment, its twisting branches reaching upward in its glass container.

"It's the glowing, right?" he said as the tree shifted from emitting a vibrant, turquoise gleam to radiating a neon yellow light. "It got me when I first saw it too. Genetic engineering does some crazy stuff. The rich use them for light and decoration these days, designing newer, more intricate trees constantly. The carpet's actually grass."

Dune glanced uncertainly down at what he thought was carpet caressing his feet. "It's white," he said.

Clive smiled. "I know. It's also absorbent and stain-resistant. Perfect for parties."

"Unbelievable," Dune said. "Are Natalie and Sage done showering?"

"They'll be with us in a moment," Clive said. "Also, your new suits of armor will be arriving in the next few minutes. Orwell Class technology with high-grade alloys and nanite reservoirs."

Dune nodded, tossing the beer cans into the recycling receptacle. "Why are you helping us, Clive? Most people would kill for the armor you're getting us and you act like it's pocket change. What is your deal?"

Clive's grin grew ever larger. "Life's nothing without a new challenge."

Dune shook his head. "You're crazy."

"No," Clive said, pulling a bottle off of the kitchen's wine rack. "I'm just unfulfilled."

He poured himself a glass of the translucent, gold-colored liquid and downed the stuff in one fluid motion. "You're not too sane yourself, Douglas," Clive said as he poured another. "I don't know many people who go it alone, pick up a rifle, and throw on battered suits of armor to take on well-rooted gangs and corrupt politicians. At least I generally hide behind stacks of paperwork and code."

"For one, I don't want to do any of that stuff. Second of all, I don't go it alone," Dune said.

"Fair enough," Clive said, finishing his second glass. "You run around with your little sister and an underpaid, uninformed hospital nurse."

Dune opened the fridge. "I need more beer."

Clive burst out laughing.

"What's so funny?" Natalie said as she entered the room, decked out in new, black tactical clothes.

"Alcoholism," Dune said.

"The look he makes when I call him Douglas," Clive said.

Dune shot him a stink eye and the informant laughed some more, trembling enough to mess up his well-gelled, curly hair.

"Leave the man alone, de Santos," Natalie said.

"Ooooh," Clive taunted. "We're whipping out the last names now?"

"I'm not whipping out anything. How's the Vanguardsman?"

"The news stream they've got going on the contacts says he's terrorizing the Lower Levels still and has killed multiple City Guardsmen," Clive says.

"Do you believe it?" Natalie said.

"I fully believe he may be terrorizing the Lower Levels," Clive said. "But killing dozens of people doesn't seem his style."

"You sure?" Dune asked. "You met him in a sewer."

"I know the kind of guy he is," Clive put his bottle of wine back in the cooler, half its content gone. "Plus, when did you start trusting Syndicate news?"

"I didn't," Dune said.

"Didn't you work with the Vanguard back in the day? I would've thought you'd be the first to trust them."

"Vanguardsmen are people," Dune said. "They can be good and they can be bad. I don't know the guy personally, just that he's strong enough to walk through walls and lift skyships. That makes me a bit nervous."

"Whether he's a good guy or not, he's our best chance to stay alive right now," Natalie said. "The more they focus on him, the better our chance of leaving the city without getting arrested. What time are we leaving?"

"Tonight at six," Dune said.

"And it's seven right now?"

Dune nodded.

"Seems a bit too long to me," Natalie said.

"We'll be fine as long as we stay in the apartment," Clive said. "I made sure of it."

Natalie looked to the older man. "What's there to do around here?"

Clive smiled. "A lot, Natalie, though probably nothing you'll enjoy. There's no secret shooting range or anything."

"Is there a gym?" Natalie asked.

"Of course there's a gym." Clive sounded a little disappointed. "The thing takes up half of the whole Lower Level."

Natalie looked to Dune. "You want to come spot me?"

"Sure," Dune agreed, rising from his perch on one of the barstools.

The pair walked through the apartment's hallways, the silky grass-carpet cushioning their new shoes as they passed piece after piece of odd, ethereal artwork.

"This place is ridiculous," Natalie said.

"Yeah," Dune agreed. "Did you hear about the new armor he ordered for us?"

"He got new armor? Where does he get the money?"

"He called in a few favors with the local Syndicate armory. Even had them custom detailed and painted. Got to make sure the Angel's dressed in her proper white and gold."

"Of course." Natalie stepped into the gym, Dune following soon after.

The floor, ceiling, and three of the walls of the gym were covered in wooden paneling, but it was different than anything Dune had seen before. Instead of a normal variation of brown or red fibers, the wood was a compressed stream of golden dust, the particles of ore each gently reflecting the warm light of the room in their own, unique way.

"What's with the gold gym?" Natalie asked.

"The wood's probably dent resistant," Dune said. "Better for parties."

"Who parties in a gym?"

"Us?"

Natalie smiled a little. "Fair enough."

The far wall was not made of the mysterious golden wood, but was one massive, smooth mirror. Dune studied his reflection, examining the bushy, brown beard and hair adorning his head.

"Maybe I should get a haircut," he muttered. "Probably be less gross after sewer-diving."

"I don't think getting a single hair cut would help you," Natalie said, loading weight onto one of the barbells.

Dune turned away from the mirror. "You're a sassy one today."

"It's probably the adrenaline," Natalie said as she lay down on the bench press. "Crazy morning."

"That's a good word for it, crazy. You almost got yourself killed. You gotta learn to back down sometimes."

"I'm not the one who couldn't hold his breath." She lifted the bar off the rack and did a few repetitions.

Dune spotted her, his hands hovering beneath the bar. "You're not gonna let me live that down, are you?"

"If we're going to talk about improvement, I'm certainly not going to pretend I'm the only one who needs improving," Natalie said, racking the bar.

He reached for a five-pound plate. "How much weight do you want to add?"

"Throw on tens," Natalie said. "You taught me well enough. Don't expect me to run from a fight if I think I can live through it."

"Yeah, sure."

"How's Sage?" he asked as Natalie finished the second set. Sweat was gathering on her brow and he caught the strain in her eyes. She'd loaded the weight on too heavy.

"She's doing her best to cope. It's a lot to handle. She's focusing on cleaning and re-stitching herself."

"I'm impressed she did so well." He finished loading on another round of ten-pound plates onto the bar. "Sad she didn't drop the medical supplies off at the safe house earlier. She would've dodged the whole mess."

"Well, she survived. That's something." She took a moment before starting the next set.

"Yeah, I guess."

"Hey, what'd you think of the Vanguardsman, by the way?"

Dune frowned a little at the abrupt change of conversation, but it'd do him no good to point it out. "He wasn't much like Vanguardsmen I've met before."

"Yeah?" She racked the barbell, rising from the plush bench. "How's he different?"

Dune envisioned the man, his fists delivering brutal blows with blissful ferocity, armor dissolving to reveal dark, brown eyes filled with hurt and hope. "He was a lot more raw than the others. Vanguardsmen I knew back in the day all moved with precision. They acted like unique pieces of the same machine, you know?" He helped Nat remove the plates from the barbell, the metallic clinking sounds reflecting off the gold-colored walls and floor. "This guy Clayton Moore isn't part of a machine."

She shrugged. "Pretty useful guy, if you ask me."

"Pretty dangerous guy. You know what kind of damage he's going to do to this city? Even if he manages not to harm a single innocent, the fact he was here is going to have everyone up in arms. People will riot, people will die, and the Syndicate will crack down again. He hurts the people we try to help just by existing."

Natalie shrugged again. "Kent didn't hurt people."

I wish we never met Kent, he thought.

She walked out of the room, leaving Dune alone with the towers of weights and a floor of gold. His sigh filled the quiet room with its melancholy weight.

How can she manage to distrust every normal person she meets, but then trust the crazy, inhuman, super soldiers? Dune thought as he followed her out of the room. He remembered Kent as well as she did. How could he not? The guy had wings. He trekked with them across Washington, helping them work their way through all sorts of dangerous terrain.

Then he died, Dune thought. *Because that's what people do when they face off with the Syndicate.*

Natalie led him all the way back to the living room where Clive and Sage were both perched on one of the plush couches. Clive leaned forward in anticipation as Sage sat in an upright fetal position, clutching an expensive pillow while gazing at the newsfeed projected onto the plane of glass suspended in the air before them. Natalie took it all in, her eyes scanning the newsfeed as it displayed one of the governor's public representatives addressing the situation. A video projected in the background, showing their new Vanguard acquaintance doing battle with City Guardsmen, sending some men soaring through the air. Others he crippled with abrupt, well-aimed blows. One guard dropped to the concrete beneath Clay's feet, the man's knee broken by a well-placed two-fingered jab. He left a permanent dent in the City Guard's suit of armor with that particular blow. Another guard flew through a nearby store's window, thrown as if he weighed less than a doll.

"What a force," Clive commented.

"We have received reports that the carrier has been working as a City Guardsman in the Lower Levels for some time now," the newscaster said to the spokesperson on screen. "What does the Governor have to say about the potential breach in infrastructure?"

Clive grinned, glee written across his face as he turned to Natalie and Dune. "I had to slip a few thousand credits into the right pockets to get that question asked."

"Why'd you do that?" Sage asked, intrigued.

"It'll keeps the Guard commissioner off-balance," Dune replied. "He looks bad and people won't trust him for a while. That makes it easier for Clive to work the system."

Clive shrugged. "Guilty as charged. I also like seeing the poor man squirm."

"Those rumors are lies and they are dangerous," the spokesman continued bluntly, pushing a few stray strands of hair into their assigned spot on his balding head. "If the carrier had been here before today, its very presence would've caused thousands of individuals to be infected with the CDT virus. Anyone who spreads such rumors will be arrested for trying to cause a disturbance of the peace and for treason against humanity."

Natalie turned to Clive. "That's you, de Santos. Treasonous truth-teller."

"I know." He rubbed his hands together in anticipation. "Isn't it thrilling?"

"The Governor wants to remind the people of Seattle we are not facing only one carrier," the pasty, thickset public representative said. "Our enemy is extinction, and it still might win if we are not united in this conflict. The system we have isn't perfect, but it's all we've got and it's our only possible way of taking back the former glory of humanity. Anyone who acts to divide us puts thousands of lives at risk."

"Yeah, whatever," Clive muttered as the screen disappeared into one of the living room's walls, leaving the living room screenless once more. Dune, however, was glancing at Sage, her green eyes filled with something dark.

"You ok?" he asked, sitting next to her. "Today's been a pretty crazy day for you."

"He makes a good argument," Sage said. "The governor, I mean."

Natalie scowled. "Not really."

"Okay, then what's your plan?" Sage asked with a shrug, releasing the pillow from her firm grip as she emerged from her curled position. "If you did manage to take down the system they've got set up, what would you replace it with?"

"We're not trying to abolish the Syndicate, Sage," Dune said.

Natalie contested. "Speak for yourself."

Dune rolled his eyes. "Most of us aren't."

"Sure about that?" Clive asked.

"Wait, you're both trying to overthrow the government?"

"Yes, Dune," Natalie said. "Get with the program."

Dune looked at her and sighed. "Never mind. Clive's crazier than I realized."

"I'm sorry," Clive apologized, "I was under the impression that you're both as tangled in this as Natalie and I are. Am I wrong? Dune, you've been in on this from the start. Sage, you've been harboring fugitives for months."

"Today's the first time I've helped with fighting," Sage said. "I'm usually the one that fixes these two up after they almost get themselves killed."

"They'll still kill you. The Syndicate has cameras everywhere," Clive said. "They've probably already looted your apartment."

"But you're a hacker, right? Can't you get me a new identity and tuck me away somewhere?" Sage asked.

"I can. But I only make profitable investments." He sipped at his glass of wine, its golden color pairing nicely with his gray-and-green outfit.

He probably planned it that way, Dune thought. *Clive cares a lot about color coordination.*

"Oh, really," Sage mocked, "like these two? No offense to Dune, but they seem like they're a bit more risk than they are reward."

Natalie scowled.

She's definitely got a point, Dune pondered.

"Could be. At least they're dedicated ones," Clive mentioned with a shrug.

"You mean Natalie's the dedicated one," Sage chuckled.

"No, they're both dedicated. Natalie's dedicated, sure, but so is Dune." Clive winked at him. "He's just got his own priority, right, Douglas? Promises to keep and all that."

Dune scowled, making Clive laugh.

"My money says she'd be less comfortable with walking away if she'd seen the vids," Natalie said.

"What vid?" Sage asked.

Natalie ignored her. "Pull up the vid and let her see."

Clive summoned the screen with a wave of his hand. The vid played after a moment as the lights automatically dimmed around them.

"What is this?" Sage asked once more.

They were observing through the lens of a body-cam mounted on a Syndicate Harness suit, giving them view of a battered, thick forest. The sky above was filled with stars, magic beacons glittering in the midst of a black abyss and shining light down on the carpet of clouds resting a short way below Clive's apartment.

Dune gazed out the windows at the sunny morning sky. *It's been a while since I've had a view like that. Maybe, if we're lucky, we'll get to see some stars before we leave tonight.*

Syndicate soldiers moved through the forest, adorned in Black Class Harnesses, all of which were different shapes and sizes. Most of the Harnesses stood only seven or so feet tall. Some were smaller, while others stood entire heads above the others like large, mechanical trolls. All had their weapons drawn and loaded.

"We close yet?" one Harnessed soldier asked. The crevices in his black Harness armor emanated dark, purple light billowing behind him like intangible, glowing smoke as they moved.

"We're about two hundred feet out." The soldier's armor radiated green light that seeped through the armor's cracks, collecting in tendrils that looked like smaller, new sprouts.

"So, it's time to gather the troops," said another.

The camera turned with the soldier, suddenly facing the one giving the commands.

Before them, perfectly framed by the screen, stood Nathan Orwell. He was the White Hart, unofficial king of the world. His Harness was unique from all the others. Instead of being plated with black-painted armor, it was clad in plates covered in radiant white. Darkness leaked out from under the plates, shadows lurking and shifting like a metallic ocean. The Hart was not adorned in the robes he usually wore over the suit. He'd chosen to wear some unnecessary extra armor, instead. The white plates of protection reflected the moonlight, making him a walking, talking star.

The trees around them rustled as more humanoid forms emerged from the underbrush. Their skin, though white, wasn't the same white as the Hart's armor. The color was closer to rice paper, but hard, like the shells of insects. Quiet, chirping noises echoed among their ranks, but their eyes were the most off-putting. Overlarge and black, they gleamed in the starlight, thousands of soulless, round skies within them.

The infected had arrived.

Dune glanced at Sage. Her eyes were wide, her lips drawn into a tight, firm line.

The soldiers in the video felt the same way, it seemed. A few of the Harnesses shifted, some tightening their grip on their firearms.

"Easy, friends." The White Hart moved forward through the ranks of soldiers and into the midst of the infected, the white, hollow sea parting to let him through as he hovered a foot or so above the earth. "They are with me."

The head soldier gave a curt nod and the other Harnessed troops did their best to stay calm. It was hard to have years of propaganda and

45

conditioning reversed in a moment. Still, they were trained, so they stood like silent toy soldiers, waiting to act as their owner desired. When the order was given, they obliged.

"Charge," the White Hart commanded, and the peaceful clearing exploded with an eruption of motion.

The Harness capturing the scene for them took off into the air, the armor blazing such intense blue it illuminated the trees around it. A few others ascended with it, filling the sky around them with different shades and types of color. The trees shifted, moving out of their way at the command of the soldier whose suit glowed green. The swarm of the infected moved like a screeching, white river of stiff flesh, some sprinting on two feet while others galloped on all four limbs. Their target was easily visible once the trees were done crawling out of their way. A derelict United States fort rested peacefully in the night, surrounded by serene beds of corn and other crops a ragtag community of survivors had planted.

Gunfire pierced the darkness of the night as the small colony saw the oncoming horde charging in the moonlight. The bullets dropped some of the diseased, spraying the innocent crops with green blood, but the swarm was endless.

The horde reached the fort in moments and began climbing the walls, the sound of their screeches forming a haunting chorus with sharp gunfire providing percussion. Some of the colonists laid down cover fire while the infirm and the children tried to escape, fleeing the fort in hijacked Army transports. The vehicles were efficiently stopped by the soldiers, their Harnesses making them more than capable of ensuring the deaths of such defenseless human beings. The screams of a few kids pierced above all other noises moments before they were silenced.

"Turn it off," Sage whispered.

Clive waved the screen away. The lights came on, revealing a scowl adorning Sage's face.

"Who were they?" she asked.

"We can't be entirely sure," Clive said. "However, I'd hazard to guess the camp was made of a mix of wanderers who happened upon the colony and leftover United States military personnel who didn't trust the Syndicate."

"Why?" Sage wiped the stray tears from her face.

"No idea," Dune cut in. "We have no clue whatsoever. The vid stops soon after that."

"I dug through Syndicate servers for weeks looking for the rest,"

Clive admitted. "I only found this clip because the soldier in the Harness sent it off to one of her mentors at a different base. She couldn't cope with it, needed someone to support her." He leaned forward, rubbing his hands together as he thought. "She died a month later. Killed in action, 'protecting' a Syndicate farm from a horde of infected. Sounds arranged, to me."

They sat in silence for a few moments, the sound of Sage's deep breaths providing the only disturbance. With her eyes closed, she pressed her hands against her lips as she slowly inhaled and exhaled through her nostrils. "Are the Governors aware?"

"Sage, the White Hart doesn't answer to the Governors," Dune said. "He owns them. We live in a world filled with infected and he's the one that keeps them out. No one says no to a man like that."

Sage grimaced.

"Feel free to leave as soon as we get to another city," he said gently. "But you've got to understand why the three of us will not be joining you."

"Let us know what your decision is before we leave," Clive said. "We'll need to prepare if you'll be joining us."

Sage stared in front of her, scowling at the wall. After a few seconds of waiting, Dune walked out, not having liked the vid much, either. He didn't get far before Natalie caught up.

"You were kind of supportive back there," she said, settling into a brisk walk by his side.

"Yeah, well, don't get used to it." Dune kept his voice low. "I just said it to keep her from running off."

"Oh, come on, Dune." Impatient, Natalie's posture was firm and unmoving. "You know as well as I do we can't sit this fight out."

"Why not?" Dune asked, turning to face her. "Let's be honest, Nat, we're not doing anyone any good here. Sure, you killed a few big-name criminals and, sure, we took out a gang or two, but that doesn't make us special!" While his voice rose in intensity, he kept its volume down to a hush. "You watched the vid, same as I did. Fact of the matter is, we're never going to be strong enough to take on the Syndicate. We could barely keep ourselves alive when we ran into small packs of infected during the Outbreak and we're messing with the organization headed by a man who can sic the entire horde on us!"

"We're stronger than we were then," Natalie said, her dark eyes hard and stubborn.

"No, we aren't, Nat," Dune replied, emphatically. "You might be stronger, but I'm not 25 anymore. I'm just a guy with a gun who's too young to be old and too old to be young."

They stood in silence for a few moments, Nat's eyes drilling holes into Dune's. Hers burned with passion, like a righteous queen roused to fury by the blasphemy of a lowly peasant.

Dune sighed, staring down in defeat. "I'll follow you to the end of the world, Nat, you know I will. I get it's hard for you. The first few years with the infected was rough for everybody and I get that you'll never totally come back from that. Neither of us will. But seriously, I promised Dad I'd keep you safe and you know how hard it is for me to keep that promise when you go chasing after your bad guys."

"They're not my bad guys, Dune," Natalie said, her voice rich with a confusingly complex jumble of emotion. "They're the world's bad guys." She stared him down for a few more moments before turning away from him.

"You'd better get ready," she said, walking back inside. "It's going to be a crazy night."

6

Clay

Things were going well enough for Clay until the fire team of Harnesses arrived. Sure, he was getting shot at, but that was nothing new.

"You've got six incoming problems," Ice said through Clay's hearlinks. "J.J.'s gonna be pissed."

"I'm not late yet."

Another few bullets deflected off his obsidian, ricocheting into the ground, a nearby wall, and one of the City Guards.

Clay scowled.

The guards were retreating; one held the line and laid cover fire while the others fell back further down the block. There'd been a whole slew of them that'd welcomed him when he came flying out of the hole in the street. He nearly landed on one. Now, the asphalt road was littered with downed City Guards, some curled into the fetal position, others clutching broken appendages.

Clay picked up a nearby manhole cover and used the thing like a shield, rushing a firing guard. "Gimme a second and I'll be out of here."

"The way it's looking right now, they'll be there before you get away," Ice said. "You could try the sewer. It's pretty easy to get out of the city through the pipes, you'd be gone in half an hour, tops."

And pull the guard back down there, right on top of the Angel and her friend. Clay dropped the guard with a well-placed jab, breaking her collarbone. She was tenacious, though, scrambling toward her dropped rifle.

"I can move faster up here. I just need a skycar." Clay plucked the gun from the guard's hands, bending the barrel into a U shape.

"Yeah, well, you'd better get closer to some, then. I can't hack any with how far you are from the nearest parking pad."

"Then tell me where to go and I'll get in range."

"Alright, alright, head north. It's away from the Harnesses, so it'll buy you a bit of time."

Clay ran up the road, taking a rifle from one of the semi-conscious guards as he went. The city still blared with flashing red lights and alarms reverberating in Clay's chest, but he thought he could still hear the footsteps over it all. Each one was like a massive jackhammer thudding into the concrete.

They're not being discreet anymore, he thought, running away from the thunderous steps.

"Twenty yards northeast," Ice directed. "Closest skycar is a blue Reyes. I've got the code ready, so I'll have it on for you in a minute."

"You're a wizard," Clay said, "but a minute may not be soon enough."

"It won't be," J.J. cut in on the other end. "And you'll be in a world of hurt."

"Oh," Ice muttered. "Hey J.J."

"Ice, has he been there the whole time?" Clay asked, punching a hole in the nearest building. If he was lucky, he might be able to get a floor or so up, maybe lose the Harnesses in the urban maze of offices and rooms.

"No, I have not. I simply observed Ice was missing and figured I'd find him in the back of the transport."

Clay finished tearing through the building's outer wall and was greeted by the fearful face of a graying, old man. He was hunkered under what appeared to be his own office desk.

"Sorry," Clay whispered, and turned away. *Guess I won't lose them in the building. Guy would probably be killed, either by the Harnesses or by exile.*

"What's going on, is Moore getting beat?" a voice said through Clay's hearlinks.

"No, I'm doing quite all right, May." Frustration was creeping into his tone as he hid himself behind one of the other nearby skycars, his firearm ready. He did not need this reunion at the moment. "J.J.'s worried about me."

"Of course he is," May said. "You get yourself into trouble all the time."

"What's Clay doing?" another voice asked, this one softer and a little brighter.

"Just doing my job, April," Clay said quietly. "Who's driving y'all's transport, anyway?"

"Chik's got it," Ice mentioned. "Problems are 100 feet out."

Clay could feel it. The ground was shaking under his feet. "How much longer till my car's set?"

"Thirty seconds," Ice answered.

"You're screwed, Moore," May chimed in.

Clay grimaced. "You know, May, I was really hoping we could have a nice conversation for once after you got back from Atlanta."

"You've got to get your act together before that's ever going to happen."

Rude, Clay thought.

Two Harnesses lumbered into view, their huge, silver frames filling a fair amount of the street. He opened fire on the two of them, clipping them with a few bullets. Hopefully, he could keep their attention away from the old man's office to keep the gentleman from being suspected of infection.

One of the two Harnesses aimed a large metal weapon in his general direction.

"Um, that's a laser cannon," Ice said.

"You've got to move, Clay," J.J. ordered.

"Yep, I know." Clay rolled right as a blast of pure, white light punched straight through the air. He ducked into a nearby alley, glancing in the direction the Harness had fired. A large hole had been melted straight through an apartment building.

No way that didn't hit somebody, he thought. Another ray of brilliant light exploded out one of the alley walls, only a few feet from him. It burned through the cement like it was paper.

Yeah, that was too close.

"Five seconds before we've got an online skycar," Ice said.

"Beautiful." Clay felt more thudding steps. *The other Harnesses, no doubt.*

"He can't make it five seconds," May said. "He's got a glass jaw."

"May," Clay interrupted. "I really need you to shut up." He glanced around the alley, thinking.

This'd better work, he thought.

He jumped up, planted his feet on a nearby wall, and launched himself headfirst at one of the behemoths, shooting through the air like a bullet. He flipped just before he reached the war machines, his obsidian-reinforced heels firmly planting themselves in one of the Harness's breastplates. The collision knocked the Harness backward, its huge arms flailing to keep it from falling.

Press the advantage, Clay's instincts said as he hit the ground.

He leapt upward once more and landed a solid uppercut into the silver suit of armor, knocking it on its back. He only got two good hits on the prone Harness before he had to roll away, narrowly avoiding yet another round of lasers from his other opponent.

They're too slow to be half-decent at shooting. He sidestepped one laser, then ducked to evade another. *They're just annoying. Keeping me busy, slowing me down.*

"The skycar's online," Ice said.

"You're a glorious, beautiful man," Clay replied with a grin.

"Well, I mean, of course," Ice said. "Still, it's nice to hear someone else say it."

Clay smiled. "Give me a second and I'll be flying out of here."

May grumbled, making Clay roll his eyes.

He ducked under the next laser, then lunged, hitting the still-standing Harness's knee with the hardest right hook he could muster. The leg buckled and Clay dealt a hearty, flying kick to the armor's chin, straining its neck. Finally, he wrapped his hands tightly around the cannon mounted to the thing, planted his feet into its shoulder, and pulled. The laser cannon came free with the crunching and squealing of steel.

Eat that, May, Clay thought.

"Watch your eight and four o'clock." Clay took J.J.'s orders and rolled to the right, dodging the crossing beams of condensed light. He swept one of the Harnesses' legs with two quick, hard kicks, crushing its cannon.

"You still got it, man!" Ice cheered. "You should see April's face, she's got that little smile she used to smile when she'd see you!"

"Hey, leave my sister alone," May said.

Clay could've laughed. *Feels like the good times.* It almost felt like he was back in training, methodically dismantling sparring automatons. Ducking, dodging, kicking, punching, and tearing. Soon enough, he stood over the motionless frames of two cannon-less Harnesses.

"Good job," April said.

"Thanks." An old feeling stirred in him like a grizzly coming out of hibernation, until something hit him square in the back, sending him sprawling.

Of course, Clay thought. *Couldn't just be happy.* He landed on his face, hard. Someone placed a heavy foot on his back, pressing him into the concrete.

"As an enforcer of Syndicate law, I order you to stay down," the owner of the foot said. "But, as someone who lost a lot of people to the plague, I beg you to get back up so I can hit you again."

Clay scowled, glancing to the side. The speaker's other foot was off to the side, adorned in black armor, blood-colored light seeming to ooze from between the plates of armor.

Black Class Harness, Clay thought. *Not too well trained, though. Idiot's used to being the strongest around.* Supposed security was the weakness of the Black Class, in his experience.

He punched his attacker in the ankle as hard as he could. Most combatants' armor and bones would've crumpled with the blow, but a full-on Black Class Harness wasn't most combatants. The ankle held. So, he punched it again.

"I'd stop if I were you, this Harness isn't gonna give." The foot on Clay's back pressed down harder. The concrete beneath him cracked. Clay strained, his head aching with the concentration it took for him to maintain his obsidian.

"Told you," May said through the hearlinks. "He's got a glass jaw."

"It's obsidian," Clay grunted, punching the Harness in the ankle once more.

The joint gave.

The pilot in the Harness screamed, and Clay didn't blame them. Their foot was probably a complete mess inside the dented, broken armor. They fell to the side, clutching the broken joint as if they hoped to pry it back into place.

Clay stood. "Ice, direct me to the car."

"Yeah, okay, it's about a hundred yards out. Just turn around and head straight on."

"Will do."

Clay watched the Harness as it writhed on the ground. The pilot had managed to break off a piece or two of armor and blood was starting to flow, pooling on the gritty cement.

Clay sighed. "Sorry."

"Go to hell," the Harness's pilot whimpered.

Clay stood and watched them for another moment. The soldier within the Harness continued to break off pieces of the ankle's mechanism as the pool of blood continued to grow. They even threw a bloody chunk of metal at him.

"You need to move, Clayton," J.J. commanded.

"Yes, sir."

Clay turned and ran, reaching the skycar in a little more than five seconds. It was already running, its headlights cutting white light through the flashing red previously illuminating the city. Alarms still blared and, as Clay opened the door and sat, he wondered how many people in the city would deal with hearing loss after today.

"You've got a bogey coming in hot, Clay," Ice said.

The skycar was already off the ground, floating weightlessly upward. Clay had it ascending as fast as possible, pressing the altimeter's throttle as far forward as it would go.

"Another silver or a flying Black Class?"

"Flying Black."

"It's a big guy," May chimed in.

Clay turned the skycar and darted in the direction of the nearest city exit, pressing the acceleration into the floor. "Ice, you have a visual?"

"They're moving too fast. I'm gonna have to freeze a frame off of a city camera. Hold on a second."

Clay drove silently. The city alarms were giving him a headache.

"THETA PROTOCOL IS NOW IN EFFECT. WARNING: A CARRIER HAS BREACHED THE QUARANTINE ZONE. REPEAT: A CARRIER HAS BREACHED THE QUARANTINE ZONE."

Ice swore through the hearlinks.

"What, what is it?" Clay asked. He got his answer as the skycar came apart at the seams, something hitting Clay in the back as hard as a train.

His obsidian nearly shattered on impact. He'd been relaxing his hold on the armor, letting its maintenance fade into his subconscious. He used to need to focus on it every second to maintain it and, in a way, it was bad that he'd reached a level of skill allowing him to move past that. If he'd been concentrating, his obsidian would've been fine. As it was, some cracks slithered their way through it before he stopped them. By the time he'd reasserted his hold on it, he was falling through the air, towers of concrete and metal racing past him.

"Well, peachy," Clay muttered.

"Clay, you've got a serious problem."

"Well, yeah, J," Clay said, trying to devise a plan. "I'm falling to my death."

"No, idiot!" May yelled in the background. "It's McGrath! The guy in the Harness is McGrath!"

"Oh." Clay continued tumbling through the air. "Well, screw me, I guess."

A hand stronger than steel gripped him by the back of the neck before anyone could respond.

Clay hit the first wall before he'd realized he was thrown. His eyes instinctively shut as he collided with the concrete. For a few seconds, that's all there was: wall after wall, crumbling concrete and bending rebar, a few pieces of furniture and other such things mixed in. He eventually collided with a stronger wall, or maybe just ran out of momentum. Either way, one of the walls finally brought him to a halt. Clay emerged from the debris, his obsidian barely holding. The surface of his obsidian was covered in cracks with some pieces missing altogether. His head was thudding with the effort required to maintain it all and he was pretty sure something was broken. A thick liquid was running down his skin. Clay glanced down at his hand and found the cracked, broken obsidian was dripping with blood.

That's not supposed to happen, he thought, trying to push his mind through the pain.

"I hear you don't like collateral damage, Moore," a voice said. Clay recognized it plenty well. It played over Syndicate newsfeeds all the time. Clay looked through the holes his body had made in the walls. There, on the other side of a long tunnel of wreckage and ruin floated Roy McGrath, Chancellor of North America and Aide to the White Hart on his Prime Council of Security.

"I'll tell you now, that little moment of chaos right there? That just killed ten bystanders."

Suddenly, Clay understood where the blood came from. His jaw clenched and his fists balled.

Easy, his rational side thought. *He's just getting you riled.*

So? His other side thought. *This is a losing fight.* His eyes were scanning McGrath's Harness. The black exoskeleton of metal emitted various colors, as if it contained some digital half-rainbow within. Some of it leaked a bright, vibrant blue light while the cracks in his gauntlets and boots emitted a sunset-red glow. Worst of all was the armor's visor, which blazed like a violent sun. *That's a Black Class Harness pumped full of multiple Vanguard abilities and we're in the middle of a concrete coffin filled with innocents.*

We can make it out of this, said the hopeful part of Clay's mind. *We can make it out of this without too many casualties.*

"Let's dance, pretty boy," McGrath said.

No, we can't, Clay thought.

The Chancellor was already on top of him, fist raised. One second, he was ten rooms away and the next he was in striking range. Clay ducked the right hook, landing two solid hits on the Harness's rib cage protection. McGrath didn't budge.

"Clay, you'd best kill that douchebag," J.J. growled.

I'll settle for staying alive, J, Clay thought. *You can handle your own personal business.*

Clay leaned around the next three punches, shoulders hunched and arms up in a perfect boxing stance, but the fourth jab took him straight in the forearm. Clay felt his obsidian crack despite his best effort to maintain it. The hit took him off his feet, throwing him back into that same buckled wall of concrete. Clay blessed high heaven that it held.

"Keep your arms up!" May yelled.

I did, Clay thought. *Doesn't do much good when the guy hits like that.*

Clay ducked the next jab, McGrath's fist putting a hole through the wall like it was paper before he was able to uppercut the Chancellor's armored chin. The man in the Harness hardly flinched.

"You're the worst, Roy," Clay gasped through the pain, trying to concentrate. He thought the Chancellor bristled at the sound of the name, but he didn't have much time to think about it. Roy's uppercut took Clay's obsidian facemask clean off. Clay felt his lip burst open, blood running into his mouth and down his chin. He landed on his back.

Somewhere in the other room, he heard a whimper.

He took another punch, this one to the stomach. Clay heard a loud crack and, with pain shooting through him, he didn't know if it was the obsidian or a few of his ribs. He brought his legs and arms up defensively and McGrath wailed on them. Clay was sure the Chancellor was saying something, but he couldn't hear what.

My head is going to explode, Clay thought. It was like a handful of anvils were being rammed into his cranium. *I am about to die.* He could hear the others screaming at him through his hearlinks, but they were background noise. The alarms were background noise at that point. It was just him, the pain, and the ringing in his ears.

And the screaming. The person in the room next door had stopped whimpering; they were screaming instead.

Save them! Clay's soul begged and, because it begged and because he cared, Clay tried. He kicked the Chancellor off of him, knocking him a few feet backward which, in and of itself, was more than Clay had thought he'd be able to do. Clay stood and took a deep breath, trying to reassert control over his mind and, as a result, his obsidian. Some of the spider web cracks disappeared, some of the empty gaps filled in. Then McGrath came back at him, lunging, his arm already extended to throw a wild haymaker.

He's got anger issues, Clay remembered. His ribs were throbbing in time with his head. *J said he's got anger issues. Use it, man, use it.*

The others were still screaming at him as he ducked the haymaker, many of them probably giving their conflicting approaches to the fight. They were still only background noises, though. Clay was still alone with the pain, the screams next door, and the ringing in his ears, but now his training chimed in as well.

One-two punch as you duck, it said, and Clay obliged. His fists took the Chancellor in the stomach and Clay saw the Harness-bound man flinch.

That's a win, his training said. *He'll backhand at you, now. Duck under and uppercut.*

Clay did, and the Chancellor's head whipped back with the blow's impact.

Another win. He's bringing a knee up to catch you in the ribs. Step away from him, catch it, see if you can make him lose his footing.

Clay obliged. He wasn't strong enough to get McGrath off-balance now that the Chancellor expected such a move, so he dealt a hard blow to the Harness's hip joint, hoping to get the internal workings to jam or dislocate. The Chancellor went to lock him in with one arm, likely hoping to keep Clay in close to rain a few blows on him. Clay ducked the armored, grasping arm, grabbed the Chancellor by the bicep with his free hand and attempted lifting the man again. This time, the Chancellor lost his feet.

J.J.'s yell punched through the fog and Clay's focus: "Kill the douche."

Clay was on top of him before he knew it, fists raining down on the Harness. The Chancellor had his arms up, but a few of Clay's fists found the Harness's visor, nonetheless.

Keep going, his training yelled. *Keep going!*

Clay laughed a bit of a reckless laugh, each hit fueled by years of frustration and anger. "You're slow, McGrath!" he bellowed. "You've gotten slow!"

Then the Chancellor's sun-colored visor burned bright

GET OUT OF THE WAY, Clay's training screamed, and Clay obeyed again, narrowly evading the beam of burning light that launched itself from the Harness's visor. Even still, the beam's residual heat hit him like a wave, putting him on his heels.

McGrath stood, visor still blazing. "Doesn't matter, bud," he said. "I can still put you in the ground." Then another beam flew.

GET OUT OF THE WAY, Clay's training said, but Clay knew there was someone in the room behind him. So, he planted his feet, brought his arms up, and took the beam head-on.

The heat hit him first, stiff and heavy on his skin, working its way through the obsidian. Next was the actual beam itself. Even through his crystalline coating, it felt like a hot iron, scalding him. The concentration it required to hold it off was too much. It hit his brain like a cannonball. He still heard the screaming, though he was the one screaming, now. He was burning. His nerves felt like they were being flayed, like he was being erased, layer after layer. The others weren't saying anything anymore or, if they were, he couldn't hear them. It made him sad.

It was nice for a bit, he thought. *Felt like the good times.*

Then he blacked out.

7

J.J.

J.J. had learned long ago that one of the many downsides to living in a containment suit is that no one knows how you're feeling or what you're thinking. However, he'd also realized that such a weakness was also one of the greatest strengths of his unique situation.

He sat, silent, staring at the screens in front of him, his containment suit's hulking frame filling a lot of their small skyship's command room. They showed Clay's limp body hit the ground from multiple angles, his obsidian blasting off his body like ash blown in hurricane-force winds. The others were silent, waiting for J.J. to say something.

In that moment, it was an immense blessing that they couldn't see him.

He silenced his suit's speakers with a thought and screamed within its sealed confines. With the interior as cut off from the rest of the world as it was, he could bellow and rage without anyone hearing a thing. The wail lasted a solid second or two, concealed in absolute silence. Then he took a deep breath and gave a second shriek, feeling his mouth open and his chest deflating as air rushed out of his lungs. Then he brought the speakers back online.

"Cut the feed and kill Clay's Creator contacts," he said.

Ice began tapping away at his interface.

J.J. watched the video feed for a few more seconds. McGrath approached Clay's unconscious body, rolling it over with his toe. With Clay's obsidian gone, they had a clearer view of the armor he'd stolen from his Precinct. The plating was crumpled and dented and the visor had shattered some time ago. The breastplate was steaming, marred with a dark scorch mark. It had taken the brunt of McGrath's optic blast once the obsidian had shattered.

"Everybody out of the room."

The others filed out of the room without a word. J.J. could feel the host of things May had on the tip of her tongue but she walked out without speaking a single word.

Well, at least there's that, J.J. thought. *Losing Clay's enough, as is. I'd rather not handle May as well.*

The door clicked closed behind them and he sighed, the weight of the world pressing down on him.

"Years of work and planning, gone sideways in minutes," he muttered, plugging his suit into the network of interfaces. The screens flickered back on at his bidding, displaying all the maps, plans, and information they'd attained over the years, clearly organized. The treasures of all his work, all *their* work, presented before him.

The plan's going to have to change, of course, he thought. He'd have to split them into two fireteams, now, instead of the three fireteams they'd planned for. He'd need to be in one and May would have to be in the other. With Clay gone, they were the only two who could really take a hit.

We'll have to be faster, more efficient. Ice will come with me and Chik will have to go with May. Can't have either group going without tech support. April will go with May, of course.

He frowned inside his armor. With April in the fireteam, he wanted to stick them outside, controlling the entrance into the Institution, keeping out any incoming forces, but May wouldn't let that happen, he knew.

We'll just have to be fast, he thought. *It'll be fine.*

He knew he was lying to himself. After years of work to get one of their own back, they'd just lost another. Even if they got Jaxon back now, they'd have to start all over again, searching and hunting Clay down.

And that's only if they don't suck him dry, J.J. thought. *He could be dead by tomorrow.*

It's a losing battle, his doubt said. *You'll all just die. They'll catch each one of you, drain your Abilities to make Harnesses, and kill each of you.*

He ignored it, scrolling through their schematics and plans.

You'll just lose them, one by one, it whispered to him. *Just like you lost the McAllisters.*

We can pull it off, J.J. thought back, pulling up some of his personal, secure files. *We're skilled. We're strong. We've prepared for years. We can push through.*

He opened one of the files. He'd been putting plans together throughout the day, scanning blueprints and data as Clay and the others sent it all in. This particular plan was what he'd put together in case Clay couldn't be a part of the operation, for whatever reason. Its name read Operation_Gate_Crasher: Black_Knight.

He looked over the strategies he'd devised. They'd need to change their initial approach. Instead of the more physical assault on the server room for a quick link-up to the prison's mainframe and database, they'd need to see if Ice and Chikaze could hack the place remotely, deactivate some of the defenses beforehand. They'd have to be much faster once they got into the Institution, but there'd be less resistance.

We can do this, he told himself.

For how long? His doubt said. *You've got plans for the deaths of all your best friends. You know you'll lose them.*

His teeth ground together in the nova-hot interior of his armor. He kept scrolling, kept reading, trying to drown the thoughts out with the text and maps.

You're just using them, trying to keep from losing yourself, it said.

Some loud thud sounded through the skyship, which lurched. J.J. braced himself against the walls, narrowly avoiding toppling backward. He stood and carefully turned as quickly as he could, managing to avoid scraping the walls with his armor's shoulders, then emerged from the room. There, out in the hall that ran the length of the skyship, an angry-looking May stood by a now-thoroughly dented wall. April, who had obviously been trying to calm May down, shot J.J. an apologetic look.

"What in the hell?"

The words erupted from him and his frustration, flying from his mouth. May's scowl soured in the face of them.

"Why are we still flying?" May said. "The op's off. Jaxon stays in jail."

"We're flying because the op's not off," J.J. said. "We're busting him out, so please don't crash my ship before we get there!"

May's scowl remained resolutely fixed and her fists clenched tighter, likely to compensate for the tears gathering along her eyes' edges.

Those eyes, J.J. thought. He sighed, and the burning frustration within him was extinguished.

He'd looked into those eyes the night Jaxon had been taken, the night May's parents had died. They'd been just as teary then, though her fists had been less scarred, less battered.

You're failing them again. You can't save them, you can't save anyone. Can't even save your wife.

His frustration flared again, McGrath's brash smile lingering in the back of his mind like a phantom, a lingering poltergeist. The images of his wife's corpse flicked through his mind. They were never far behind McGrath.

And now he got Clay, too.

A tear fled down May's cheek. It didn't get far before she caught it, but that one tear brought J.J. back out of it.

"We're still going to get him, May," he said. "I will never give up on him, and I won't give up on you, either."

May wiped aside another tear, scowling. "Anybody can say sappy stuff like that, Tin Man. Let's see you put your money where your mouth is." Then, before J.J. could say or do anything else, she stalked off toward the ship's small, crowded armory.

J.J. sighed, scanning the deep dent in the ship's wall. *That'll take a while to fix,* he thought.

"Sorry, J," April said. "You know how excited she's been. I think she's only realized in the past few weeks that this isn't guaranteed to work out."

"I'd hoped Atlanta would let her work out some of that," J.J. said. "Hoped she'd vent, or whatever."

April shrugged. "She definitely vented. She broke a lot of stuff. She didn't work anything out though."

Another thing you've been wrong about, his doubt told him.

"Thanks for all you've done for her, though, J.J.," April said with a smile. "Thanks for all you do for all of us."

J.J. nodded. "I'm sorry he got caught, April. Clay, I mean."

April's smile flickered, her eyes averting, and J.J. ground his teeth together. *Failed her too.*

"It's not your fault, J.J.," she said. "You've put everything you have into keeping us all together." Her smile returned in full force. "You don't owe me any kind of apology."

"Thanks, April," he said. "I appreciate it."

"Sure thing, boss man," April said. "What can I do to help?"

"Relieve Chik," J.J. said. "She's been flying for a while and I need to talk to her and Ice."

"Will do," April said, and she squeezed past him, walking down the hallway to the cockpit.

J.J. watched her go. "Thanks, April."

Don't get too excited, his doubt said. *She'll see how bad you've failed her, how bad you've failed them all. Just wait.*

8

Clay

"Moore, what do we do? Moore!"

"What?"

Clay snapped to reality in an instant. Everything hurt. His ribs, his skull, the whole gamut. The Vanguard North American Academy stood before him, its beautifully designed buildings looking as though they had descended from some other world, fallen from a happier sphere. Outside, statues of Vanguard legends stood in the middle of the main drive's roundabout, modern gods of a mortal pantheon, their eyes confident. There was only one problem.

The Vanguard North American Academy was on fire.

Not this, he thought. *Not again.*

Robin Wallace slapped him in the face. Though he hardly felt it, coated in obsidian as he was, it brought him back to sensibility.

"What's our plan?" she yelled.

They were surrounded by other trainees, twelve of them. Ramirez, Johnson and Kelbourne all were squatted to his right with some others, adorned in the gray, black, and white armor of the Vanguard. Clarke, Mbongo, Teller, and Scott waited on the left, along with some of the younger trainees. The main entryway seemed as though it were deteriorating around them, the clean walls punctured by bullet holes, furniture smoldering amidst shattered windows and splintered plaques dedicated to former trainees who'd risen to Vanguard greatness.

Clay took a deep breath, willing himself to wake up. Even as he struggled against his dream, he heard his younger self say, "We're going to split into three fireteams. Mbongo, your team will push through the buildings to the west of the main academy driveway. Make sure to keep a good view of the road—we'll need support as we move through."

"Roger," Mbongo said.

No! Clay thought. *Stay inside, stay hidden!* He tried to speak the words, he could swear he felt his mouth moving, but no sound came out.

"Kelbourne, you do the same, but on the eastern side. I'll lead Team One up the driveway," his younger voice said. "We're going to give and go from one end of the base to the other, try and take their squads as we find them. We'll need to be fast on our feet, watch each other's backs at all times. Hopefully, we can push them from the Academy."

"Copy," Kelbourne said.

The other trainees nodded, putting on brave faces. They acted like they believed his plan had some slim chance of success.

Even in his younger years, Clay had known from the start that it was a suicide mission. But what else could they do? They could die fighting or die hiding.

The teams left the Administration building, weapons ready, each one of them hunched low. Robin beat Clay to an overturned Vanguard transport, the first piece of cover in sight on the godforsaken driveway. Its wheels were on fire, filling the air with smoke and an intolerable smell. They hunched behind the mess of metal, glancing to the east and west, silently signaling to the two other teams. Clay held up one hand, three fingers raised.

Three, two, one, he signaled.

The teams burst into their respective buildings simultaneously, their heavies kicking in the doors, the others pouring into the buildings, ready to kill or be killed.

The two buildings slammed down on top of the teams, like a hammer on a coffin's final nail. Clay watched from the street, through the transport's shattered windows. He heard their screams. To this day, he didn't know who was screaming or how they could in the concrete mouse trap. He just knew the sound still made him clench and made his stomach curl as his palms went wet with a cold sweat.

"Abort," his younger self said to his team. "Get to the armory as fast as possible. Wallace and I will cover you."

Wallace stiffened at the words, undoubtedly feeling underqualified.

"We've got no other options," his younger self said to her. He looked at the trainees surrounding him. Most were only fifteen or sixteen, just recently having gone through the Procedure. Many hadn't even been through training drills yet. "If we make it to the panic room in the Armory we may be able to outlast them."

The others nodded.

"On my mark," Clay said. Then, when all were ready, he gave the fateful command: "Let's move."

The trainees leapt out from their cover, sprinting down the street as quickly as possible. Clay ran, just a few feet behind them, his hands nearly crushing his rifle's grip. Every bit of training screamed at him to get out of the street, but the Syndicate had brought a groundshifter today. As the other teams had shown, the buildings just weren't an option. Wallace glided through the air just above them, her rifle at the ready. Her Ability had been flight.

The first shot dropped Williamson, punching straight through his helmet, painting the sidewalk red. Another pierced through the shoulder of a trainee Clay didn't know. The kid dropped his weapon as he stumbled, panting, clutching his bleeding shoulder.

We're just kids, Clay thought as he watched through his youthful self's eyes. *We don't deserve this.*

Robin twisted in the air, spraying the buildings behind them as she flew. "I'll keep you covered so you can retrieve him," she said through her commlink between bursts of gunfire.

"Copy," Clay said. He picked up the wounded trainee with ease, throwing the young man over his shoulder. He ducked and weaved between burning vehicles and piles of debris, yelling orders at the trainees as they started to panic.

"Jones, keep your weapon ready! Williamson, stick with us, you've got to keep moving. Teller, what're you doing, get away from that building!"

They made it further than he'd thought they would before the shifter Harness cemented their feet into the ground. Clay, of course, broke free of his restraints almost immediately, his obsidian giving him the strength necessary. A few others, the lucky ones, were also able to steamroll through the trap. Most, however, quickly found themselves stuck, sinking into the pavement.

"Wallace, where's their shifter?" he said, searching the windows of the nearby buildings. "We've got to take him out."

"I can't find him anywhere," Robin said. She was still exchanging fire with the other Harnesses hidden in the surrounding buildings.

"I've got eyes on him," Simonson said. "First time my infrared's ever been useful."

"All right, you're with me," Clay said. He handed the wounded trainee he'd been carrying to one of their squad's big men. "Del Toro, you're in charge of leading the rest to the Armory. Stay safe."

"Yessir," Del Toro said, cradling the trainee in her large, burly arms.

Clay and Simonson burst into the office building just southeast of them. He had memories of talking with drill sergeants and teachers here. He'd borrowed *The Lord of the Rings* from the library downstairs when he'd read it for the first time. Now, he rammed through concrete walls as Simonson leapt and dodged along with him. They plunged through the building's intestines as the concrete reached out at them, trying to block their way, slow them down, or even kill them. Clay stormed through obstacles and hinderances like a roaring grizzly bear while Simonson clambered about like an ape, springing off the walls, ceiling, and whatever other surfaces were available.

"Almost there," Simonson panted.

"We've got to be quick," Clay said. He shattered a massive, concrete sledgehammer that suddenly flung itself from a nearby wall. "The others have got to be up to their necks by now."

"Wait," Simonson said, his voice growing tense.

"What?"

Clay didn't realize the building was collapsing on him until the roof above him came crashing down on his head. He gasped, struggling to breathe as he tried to push the numerous layers of concrete off his aching back. Simonson had been right next to him when the building had collapsed, but Clay couldn't see or hear him, now.

Stupid, Clay remembered thinking. *They just used that trap on the others and now I'm in it, too. Stupid, stupid, stupid.*

His younger self growled, struggling against his constraints. Then the concrete liquefied. He hung, submerged in the thick, soupy substance, unable to escape. His lungs were bursting, begging for air, his ribs protested as the heavy liquid pressed at his chest.

This is how the others felt, he thought, his younger self clawing at the mud-like cement. *Struggling until cement filled their lungs.*

He thought he'd continue to push his way out of the cement. He thought he'd continue to fight and watch others die. That's what happened in the other flashbacks and in all the nightmares, that's what had happened all those years ago.

But it didn't happen this time. He just hung, suspended, dying for air amidst the gray, gravelly mush.

It's just a dream, he told himself.

Another second went by.

It can't hurt me, he thought. *It's just a dream.*

His lungs, esophagus, and core were clenched, trying to inhale with every tendon and each strand of muscle. Still, another second passed without a breath of air.

I'm going to die, he thought.

Black was pressing in on his periphery. His muscles were going weak, his fingers and toes feeling numb, feeling cold. The cold and the darkness pushed in on him.

His mind was a firework show. Regrets, fears, hopes, they all burned within him, the desperation of a slowly dying soul.

I can't die today, he thought. *Not yet, the world's still such a mess. I'm still such a mess.*

The cement didn't care. He could hardly see. His limbs were limp at his sides.

The first breath of air came as a surprise. He gulped it in before he'd realized there was air to breathe. The cement still pressed around him, though, still limited his movement.

That's not right, he thought. Nevertheless, he took another deep breath, some of his strength starting to return.

The cement dissolved away from him, glittering like effervescent sand. The pain, however, lingered. He gathered his surroundings slowly, giving himself a moment to catch his breath. He was suspended in the air, his legs and arms dangling. Blank white walls and thick glass windows surrounded him. The room was devoid of any sound. Some kind of a mask was on his face, covering his nose and mouth. He scanned the room surrounding his cell as subtly as he could. It was empty, except for one man.

Unless he was mistaken, the Chancellor of North America stood on the other side of the window behind him. His Harness's lights gave him away.

"How're we feeling, champ?"

McGrath's voice sounded as though he were whispering in Clay's ear. That's when it clicked in Clay's head.

They've got me wearing Creator contacts and hearlinks, he thought. *Probably showed me footage from my Vanguard armor camera feed.*

Then, with a crack of the ribs, he found himself face-down on the cold, white floor.

There's the renowned Syndicate gravity manipulation, he thought. *Not a very gentle touch.*

"Nice system, huh?" McGrath said. "I hear the restraints are great for dampening Abilities."

"Evening, Chancellor," Clay wheezed.

He couldn't see the man anymore. His only view was of the polished, white tile that lined the cell's floor, his face digging into its cold, hard surface, his limbs splayed out around him. His chest protested to the pressure, pain shooting through his ribs.

"Spunky even when you're beat and strung up," the Chancellor said. "It's too bad you're gonna die, Moore. You'd be a fun guy to work with."

"Thanks, I think," Clay said. He strained his eyes, but still couldn't see his captor. He could envision McGrath, though. The Chancellor had been all over the newsfeeds for years now. He had an ever-so-slightly crooked nose, the kind that most friendly, crazy uncles have. His eyes were a blazing blue. Many women and, undoubtedly, some men whispered about them throughout North America.

Who'd have thought Beelzebub looked so pretty, Clay thought.

McGrath walked around the cell until he stood just within Clay's line of sight. They watched one another in silence for a moment, a massive, cocky grin sprawled across the Chancellor's face as he shook his head.

"You really know how to get a party going, don't you?" he said. "Manage to work yourself into the City Guard, then tear half the city apart in a day. You've scared the socks off of people."

The large man pulled up a plain, metal chair and took a seat, placing his Harness's helmet on the floor. "Honestly, I loved watching it all. The destruction of the status quo, the fear in everyone's eyes, the blood and adrenaline pumping through the whole city's veins as they fight, hide, and scream. It's been years since I was this excited."

I'm glad I'm entertaining, Clay thought.

"So, why'd you do it?" McGrath said. He leaned forward as he asked like some predator, tapping a few buttons that lit up on the glass surface of Clay's cell. "I'll even ease up the gravity for you so we can talk."

"My name is Clayton William Moore," Clay said when the gravitational pressure lessened. "I am Vanguard number 13118."

Clay thought he saw McGrath's blue eyes glint gleefully. "Ah, come on Moore, don't lock up so soon. We've got a long time together. It'll be boring if you whip out Vanguard protocol so soon!"

Clay said nothing.

"Here, I know what'll help," McGrath said, tapping the glass surface a few more times. "I've got someone you'll want to meet." Clay craned his neck, straining to get a better view.

Then his face appeared out of nowhere. Sure, it was a few years younger than the face he had now. His younger eyes radiated a lot more hope and his hair was glossy and recently cut.

"Please, state your name," a chipper voice said from off-screen.

Mr. McAllister, he thought. The sound of the man's voice cut old scars open all over again.

"Clayton William Moore, sir," the younger Clay said. His lips tentatively turned upward in an excited smile.

"You were pretty polite back then, Moore," McGrath said. His eyes were fixed on the screen, like a cat homing in on a particularly juicy mouse.

Mr. McAllister and Clay's younger self had moved on.

"Where are you currently living, Mr. Moore?" McAllister asked.

"Just outside of Dallas, sir," Young Clay said.

"Suburban home?"

"No sir, my family's got a small farm. We're just outside a pretty nice neighborhood, though."

"You were an anxious kid, huh?" McGrath said, glancing at Clay. "Seems like you couldn't figure out whether or not it was okay for you to smile. Excited to join the good, old Vanguard?"

Shut up, Clay thought.

"Why do you want to join the Vanguard Initiative, son?" Mr. McAllister said.

"I want to help people, sir," Young Clay said. Clay frowned a little as McGrath chuckled at the answer, his laughs mocking the fragile innocence displayed onscreen.

"How long did that last, Clay?" McGrath said as the recording continued to roll. "Did you make it through training before you realized you were just going to be a dressed-up, glorified killer? Or did the Outbreak help you realize that?"

We both know the Outbreak's not on me, McGrath, Clay thought.

"Your examinations and evaluations all check out, so that's good," Mr. McAllister said. "You ready for the training and work that goes into this?"

"Absolutely, sir," Young Clay said.

"You've been notified of the risks involved? You know the Procedure doesn't take for everyone, right?"

"Yessir."

McGrath smiled, shutting off the video. "Were you ready, Clay?" he said. "Were you really? If you were that kid now, knowing what you know, would you still sign up?"

Clay closed his eyes, stifling a frown.

"Oh, don't go back to sleep just yet, Moore," McGrath said.

Clay's restraints sent a brief, electric shock through him, forcing him to open his eyes again. He kept himself from crying out at the pain, though he was sure he'd jumped in surprise.

Stupid, he thought. *Should have been expected that. Can't allow him to surprise me so easily.*

"There we go!" McGrath rejoiced. "There are the dark, handsome eyes I want to see. You can't go to sleep just yet, Moore. We've still got all sorts of questions to go through in our little interview. Are you ready?"

Clay said nothing.

After a few seconds, another electric shock ran through him.

"Ready," Clay grunted.

"Excellent," McGrath said. He reached over, picking an interface off the ground beside his chair and cleared his throat.

"Did you think you'd save them, Clay? The trainees, I mean. You fought like a devil, I'll give you that, but did you think it'd do you any good?" He tapped the interface's screen as he spoke. An image appeared on Clay's glass cell wall. A dozen or so bodies lay lined up on the North American Vanguard Academy's front drive. A number of the bodies were hardly more than a bloody mangle of crushed armor. A few, though, like Wallace's, were in better condition, having been downed by a bullet instead of being mangled by a Harness crushed under a mountain of concrete.

Clay closed his eyes. *Didn't know they gathered them up for group photos like that,* he thought.

Another electronic shock went through him. He opened his eyes again, though he managed to avoid jumping at the jolt.

"You were outnumbered, outclassed, and outmaneuvered at every turn. The Academy's staff and personnel had already been detained and removed to secure prisons. You kept fighting anyway. What was the point?"

Clay didn't say a word.

"Then there's this guy."

Jaxon appeared onscreen, crouched in the middle of a spotlight. The camera that had filmed him looked down from above, peering through a hole in the ceiling of the warehouse he was in.

Atlanta, Clay thought. He knew that warehouse. It was the one they had left behind all those years ago, the warehouse Jaxon refused to leave behind, the warehouse where the McAllisters had died.

Jaxon's eyes were wide and crazed, his teeth bared like he was some war-wild animal. Sweat glistened on his face and the patches of chest peered through his devastated armor. One of his arms hung limp by his side, blood trickling through his teeth. Even still, he held a rifle in his good hand and was in motion, about to dive behind cover or something of the sort. The ground around him was littered with the bodies of Syndicate soldiers.

"What a guy." A frustrated tone crept into the Chancellor's voice. Clay smiled.

Jaxon was moving as the Chancellor spoke. He pounced, leaping out of the spotlight and disappearing beneath a piece of the rooftop. Flashes pierced the darkness of the warehouse, gunshots in the ruin's shell, a different type of light piercing the night. An explosion shook the interior.

"You know, we didn't even know it was him, at first, he was so decked out in armor and all that," McGrath said. "Most Vanguardsmen are pretty easy to identify. They shoot fire? We've got a list for that. Lift buses? There's a list of those guys, too. We only figured out that it was Mr. Stihl after we shot him a ton. Being unkillable is a bit of a subtle Ability."

The camera angle changed. The new camera was mounted on a silver-class Harness's breastplate. Jaxon was facing off with the war machine, dodging from side to side, firing at the cannon mounted on its shoulder.

Trying to damage the ranged weapon, Clay thought, thinking back to his own recent confrontation with silver Harnesses. *Great minds think alike.*

One of the weapon's beams of light caught Jaxon in his good arm, leaving him with only his two legs.

Jaxon was unphased. He charged the Harness, dodging the next two beams and leaping up onto the mechanical armor's breastplate. Clay realized his friend had a trigger in his mouth he hadn't yet noticed in the dim lighting. His eyes widened.

No way, he thought.

Then Jaxon bit down. There was a bright flash of an explosion and the camera feed went dead.

He blew himself up, Clay thought.

The Vanguard scientists had warned Jaxon about explosions back in the day. They were certain he'd come back if he was shot in the head or if he bled out. He'd come back from all of that stuff. Explosions were a different matter, though, particularly if he was at the epicenter.

They didn't know how his anatomy would react. Basically, as Clay understood it, they'd told Jaxon that they could discern that he wasn't really human anymore, genetically, but figuring out what he'd become was "a matter of speculation."

The life of Vanguardsmen, Clay thought. *Lots of speculating scientists.*

"Time and time again, you try and fail," the Chancellor said. "You lose people constantly. We could talk about your family. That's another grisly tale of loss, right? But, really, there's only one question I want to ask at this point: What on Earth's keeping you going? Why are you in Seattle?"

"My name is Clayton William Moore. I am Vanguard number 13118."

"Come on, Clay," McGrath said. "Every time you say that, I'm supposed to turn up the gravity setting." Sure enough, Clay could feel the power that pulled him downward increasing, pushing his bruised face further into the ground. The pain in his ribs grew more intense. "Just give me what I need and you won't hurt too bad before you're killed."

Doubt it, Clay thought.

"Again," McGrath said, smile still affixed. "Why are you in this city?"

"My name is Clayton William Moore," Clay said again. "I am Vanguard number 13118."

"No, you're not, Clay," McGrath said. He laughed. Clay didn't like his laugh. It was spiteful, giddy. "The Vanguard was forcefully disbanded by the Syndicate years ago. You're nobody. You're a dead man. Even worse, you're a menace to society! Why try so hard? Don't make this so difficult for yourself."

"Name is Clayton William Moore. I'm Vanguard 13118."

McGrath sighed dramatically, falsely disappointed as Clay's body was pressed harder into the careless floor beneath him. "Come on, give me an answer I can work with so we can both move on."

Oh, I'm sorry, Clay thought through the pain, *am I inconveniencing you?*

"Why did you come to Seattle, Clay?"

"Clayt'n James Moore," Clay gurgled. It was hard to breathe, now. "Vanguard. 13. 118."

The gravity increased again. "Give me another answer, Moore. No one can keep this up. You keep holding out on me, your own weight will crush your rib cage like it's a bunch of twigs."

"Turn't up, M'Grath," Clay spat.

McGrath smiled shaking his head. "Spunky to the end," he said.

The gravity went up a notch and, with a sickening pop, Clay's shoulder dislocated, pulled out of place by the force pulling him downward.

"You want to be a martyr, don't you, Moore?" McGrath said with a smile. "You want to make a hero out of yourself."

"No."

"Yeah, you do," McGrath said.

"No," Clay said. "Don't."

"Then why don't you give me the info I need so you can die easy?"

Clay drew a deep breath, straining to look over at the Chancellor. "W'll both die. N'ly d'ff'rnce, I die g'd."

He spoke more confidently than he felt.

"An honorable death," McGrath said. He reached down, retrieving his helmet from the floor, then reaffixed it onto his head. He opened the door, turning his back on Clay's bruised body. "We'll help you get that, Moore. We're good at dealing out honorable deaths."

You don't get it, McGrath, Clay thought as the door closed. His thoughts rang through the silent cell. *It's got nothing to do with dying. It's got nothing to do with being a martyr. Just want to be a good person.*

Something clicked in the mask he was wearing and Clay realized he couldn't breathe. He lay there, immobile, unable to speak as he slowly suffocated.

He passed out, silent as the grave.

9

Dune

"No," Dune said emphatically. "No way, that's not even kind of tempting."

"Oh, come on, Douglas," Clive said.

Natalie loaded a few more firearms into Clive's rather large skycar. They were standing and moving about the landing pad attached to Clive's apartment, preparing for their departure from the city. The pad jutted out over one of the gaping holes that allowed the upper levels access to the rest of Seattle. The sky and moon presided over their heads. It was the first time Dune had breathed fresh air in years, air that hadn't first been pumped through miles of vents.

It's too exposed, he thought. Another City Guard skyship flew by. The small skyships had been periodically flying over the top levels all night. Lots of craziness had gone on and it seemed that the Guard wanted to make sure no one in the upper levels got any ideas about leaving.

Clive still had the image pulled up on his mobile's screen. The Vanguardsman Clayton Moore stood between two Harness-bound soldiers, one of his eyes painfully swollen closed by the bruising that coated part of his face. "These types of opportunities only come once in a lifetime."

"Yes, and sane people ignore them," Dune said. He tossed his bag full of clothes into the skycar. "I don't know the guy, and even if I did, we can't help him. We couldn't handle one Harness. He'll have a whole team of them guarding him."

Clive's stubborn grin refused to budge. "It's a beautiful challenge, isn't it?"

Dune looked his smirking associate in the face, unmoved. "No, it's suicide."

"I've got a plan," the older man said, rolling his eyes. "It's not suicidal, trust me."

"What's your plan, Clive?" Natalie said, cutting through Dune's upcoming retort.

"I thought you'd never ask," Clive said. He shot Dune a smug look and began tapping away on his mobile's screen until, eventually, he reached what he was looking for.

"Take a look at this," he said, handing the mobile to Natalie as she leaned against the skycar's hood.

Dune craned his neck, straining to see the image on the mobile's screen. "That's not a plan, Clive. That's a map."

"A pretty small map, too," Sage said as she walked by. She deposited the container of ammunition she had been carefully carrying into one of the skycar's seats.

"Let the man explain," Natalie said.

Clive paused for dramatic effect, eagerly looking into each of their eyes, Sage joining them as they stood around the mobile. She and Dune glanced at one another. Sage rolled her eyes.

"You're looking at the floor plans for Syndicate Weapons Cache 24168," Clive said. "It's concealed two levels below us and it contains five Black Class Harnesses."

Dune took a very deep breath as a few pieces of well-chosen profanity fell from Sage's lips. *This is a dangerous road,* he thought.

"You have the access codes?" Natalie said. Her eyes were filled with hunger.

Silence hung over the four of them for a few seconds. Clive smiled, drinking in the attention.

"I do," he said.

This is officially above my pay grade, Dune thought. He glanced at Sage and saw the same fear he felt weighing down his stomach reflected on her face, the weight of regret painting over her green eyes with sorrowful colors.

"We can break him out," Clive said.

Clive's confidence made Dune feel sick. He sensed Natalie's gaze surveying him and looked down to meet her piercing, dark brown eyes.

This is what got Kent killed, Dune thought. *This whole "noble drive" to save people.*

"I'm in," Natalie said.

He scowled, staring her down. She stared back. Dune could sense Sage watching them and could see Clive's grin widen as he watched their silent battle.

Natalie didn't back down. She never backed down.

Dune sighed, then nodded. "Then I guess I am, too," he said.

The things we do for family.

Sage looked at all of them as if they'd just declared they were flying to the moon. "I'm not!" she said. "That's absolutely insane!"

"Oh, come on, Sage," Clive said, "You already faced off with Harnesses today and you survived just fine."

"Thanks to that carrier or Vanguard or whatever!" Sage said, her voice incredulous. "Now he's captured and you're going to raise the stakes? No thank you, this is where I get off the—"

"Good," Natalie said, cutting off the nurse's rant. She pushed away from the skycar's hood, standing at her full height so she could look down on the nurse. "We need someone to fly the skycar, anyway. You'll drop us off, then pick us up at the rendezvous point in the skycar. We'll fly you to some city where you can start a new life." She tossed the redheaded woman the skycar's key fob. "Sound good?"

"No, it doesn't." Sage looked to Dune, silently begging for help. He began conspicuously checking to make sure all the firearms had their safeties on, avoiding her gaze. Clive was busy "working" on his mobile.

"Well, that's tough," Natalie said. "It's the way things are going to be."

"It's really not, though." Sage's voice had gone hard, resolute. "You do what you want, but I'm not going to go head-to-head with Syndicate soldiers twice in a day."

Natalie smiled. It wasn't a kind smile, or a caring smile. It was the smile of a fox about to plunder a hen's nest.

Hate that look, Dune thought.

"If you're not going with us, Sage, what will you do?" Natalie asked. "Stay in Clive's apartment? They're already looking through indexes of his belongings."

Sage folded her arms and Dune knew she was done for. Folding one's arms is a great way to signal insecurity. He'd learned that long ago, and so had Natalie, whose eyes glinted at the sight.

"Sure, this apartment should be pretty hard for the Syndicate to trace back to Clive," Natalie said. "As I understand it, he brought it through a shell company owned by another shell company that works for a shell company linked to his bank account. They won't find the apartment tonight, I don't think. They'll arrive tomorrow. If you don't leave with us in the skycar, you won't leave. Your face has already been broadcasted to every set of Creator contacts in Seattle. You won't last a minute on the streets without being seen and caught. You've got no money to pay off smugglers. Your accounts are definitely frozen, by now."

The nurse took a deep breath, her scowl severe enough to curdle milk. For a second, no one said anything.

"Get in the skycar," Natalie said as she turned to the vehicle and expectantly sat in the passenger's seat.

Sage stood unmoving for a second, glaring after Natalie, then plodded at a rebelliously slow pace to the skyship, banishing herself to the darkest corner of the back seat.

Clive grinned. "Fantastic!"

Dune frowned as he got into the skycar. *I'm about to die,* he thought, the automated doors closing behind him. *My stubborn little sister's officially lost all sense, and I'm going to die.*

10

Natalie

Natalie sat in the passenger's seat, loading up another magazine.

Clive sat next to her, chatting up a storm and messing with his mobile interface as they flew through the city's innards. Usually, Natalie would complain about inattentive driving, but she'd seen Clive navigate the city's inner workings before. He could make a sharp, 90 degree turn with precision while in the middle of a hack. She wasn't sure what it was about the guy, though if she had to guess she'd say it had something to do with years of practice and his ADHD. He could multitask like no one else.

Dune and Sage didn't say a word in the back. Natalie couldn't see them, but she had no doubt the nurse was giving her brother a vicious stink eye. Dune would be moping, trying not to look at her, acting like he'd rather be anywhere else.

And yet, he always comes, she thought. *He always mopes, but he always comes. He needs this.*

Her brother had been getting soft after they'd first arrived at the quarantine zone. Sure, he got a job and stayed busy during the day. When the nights came, though, he was directionless, bored, or drunk. Now, reluctant as he was, he had purpose. Though he might be a little buzzed.

Stupid that Clive gave him beer, she thought. *Risky move. We need him at full capacity.*

It'd become apparent over the years that the informant was smart, extremely useful, and sometimes a little too insightful. He'd never reined in his confidence though.

Might get one of us hurt, she thought.

Beside her, he rattled off plans and strategies like a song played at twice its normal speed. "We've got a lot of options to choose from," he said, scrolling through the bunker's inventory. "There's two strength armors, one flight, and two with unique Abilities."

"What are they?" Natalie said.

"Speed and invisibility," Clive said. He listed off the suits of armor as if they were ordinary components of his everyday grocery list. It made her smile just as much as it made her wary.

"I'll take invisibility," she said. *Dune will appreciate that. Staying out of the way and all that.* She'd rather fly, like Kent had. There'd be time for that another day. Today they were going to work.

"I'll wear the speed Harness," Clive said. "Dune, I think it would be best if you wore a strength suit, that way we've got a bruiser to back us up if we need one."

"Sure, I'll take the hits for y'all," Dune said. If Clive recognized the mingled resentment and resignation in his words, he didn't show any indication. Instead, he continued his plans and speculation.

"I wonder how steep the learning curve will be," he said to Natalie. "Like, will you be able to turn invisible and, even if you can, will you be stuck that way?"

"We're so screwed," Dune whispered. Natalie barely managed to hear him over the older man's prattle. Sage hissed something back that shut him up.

Tough cookie, Natalie thought.

Natalie clicked the last bullet into her magazine. She loaded one into the chamber and rested her assault rifle on her lap.

Clive paused his theoretical rambling. "Please keep chambers empty in the skycar. As much as I enjoy hacking into the governor's bank accounts, it'd be wasteful to humiliate her cybersecurity guys just to repair a little shattered window."

Natalie rolled her eyes and emptied the rifle's chamber.

"Thanks." He turned toward the back of the car. "If you're both done sulking, I've got a game plan drawn up."

"Let's hear it," Dune said.

Sage said nothing, but Clive pressed on anyway.

"I'm going to hack the city's security camera feeds five seconds before drop off, that way they won't see us coming," he said.

"Are you going to put it on a loop?" Dune said.

"No, loops are too noticeable," Clive said. "I'll make it so we don't show up on the feed. Use the system's identification protocols to identify us and erase us from the image."

"You can do that?" Natalie said. *Would've been handy to have that before now.*

"This is the big time, Nat," the old man said. "We're busting out the big kid toys."

Natalie frowned a little. Dune was the only one who called her Nat, and she didn't like being compared to a child.

"We'll breech through the southern entrance," Clive continued. "It's less guarded and the hallways leading to the cache itself are more of a straight shot. We can punch through quick, then get out."

"What am I doing?" Sage said.

"Flying out of the city immediately," Clive said. "Meet us 20 miles north of the quarantine zone's northern skygate. There are files in the skycar's system that will identify it as the personal vehicle of one of the generals in the Las Vegas quarantine zone. You just dropped him off here so he can spend some time with his mistress. You've got to get back before his wife notices. There's a uniform in the back of the car. Sure, such a trip's illegal, but they'll give the guy and his staff a pass."

"And if the uniform doesn't fit?" Sage said. "You only just met me today."

"The uniform will fit," the informant said. "I've got your measurements."

"I never gave them to you," Sage said.

The old man shrugged. "I've got an automated sewing assembly in my house. Security system took everyone's measurements when they walked in the door."

"Useful as that is, Clive, it's creepy," Natalie said.

"Definitely creepy," Sage said.

"Sorry to interrupt," Dune said, "but if Sage is leaving, how are we meeting up with her? There's no way we'll get out on foot."

"Of course not," Clive said. "I paid off a guard to leave a small transport running on the landing pad just north of the position." He gestured at a homemade mechanism on the dashboard. "I'll have this on me when we're leaving. It sends out a signal that'll open any skygate."

"When do they move the Vanguardsman?" Natalie said.

"They'll move him in half an hour," Clive said.

"How do you get all of this information?" Sage said. "You do a pretty good job of making it seem like you know everything."

Natalie smiled a little. *Perceptive question.*

"Years of work and insane amounts of manipulation have gotten me where I am today," Clive said. "Hence the utter disregard for social norms."

Natalie frowned. He never gave a straight answer when asked about his hacking.

"That's obviously unhealthy," Sage said.

"Trust me, I'm well aware of that," Clive said flatly. "Now, how about we decide an official rendezvous point?"

Natalie heard Sage huff in the back seat.

"I'm thinking we'll intercept Clay's prison transport just after it leaves Seattle through the northern skyport on the lower levels," Clive said. "I should be able to remotely cut the lights inside, then we can drop Dune onto the roof and have him make an opening for us. If all goes well, the skyship won't make it more than ten miles into Old Seattle."

"So I should be ten miles north of the skyport, then," Sage said.

"Twenty, just to be safe," Clive said.

Natalie heard a magazine click into place and a shotgun racking in the backseat. Dune was ready.

"Keep the chamber empty while in the skycar," Clive said. "We're almost there."

Go time, Natalie thought.

"What's our ETA?" she said. She clipped a few grenades to the magnetic bandolier on her new suit of armor.

"One minute," Clive said. The skycar banked to the left, turning onto the bunker's street. The informant's fingers zipped around his mobile's surface. Natalie had no idea what he was doing. She'd asked him to teach her once or twice, but he always put her off and said there'd be a better time.

Shame to miss the opportunity, she thought. *Syndicate doesn't let anyone learn code, these days.*

"Pass me some extra shotgun shells," Dune said from the back.

Natalie turned and tossed him a few. He'd already put his helmet on. His new armor was pitch black and unscathed. Much nicer than the stuff he used to wear.

We've come a long way, Natalie thought.

"I'm guessing the target's buried somewhere in that," Dune said, pointing at a sort of column of structures off to the right of the skycar. The stack of structures, buildings, and landing pads ran from the bottom of the city level to the ceiling above.

"Yep," Clive said.

"Are there housing complexes built into the column?" Sage said.

"There are a few," Clive said. "Shouldn't be too much of a problem, though. It's a tough neighborhood. Local civilians will be used to the sound of gunfire. Should be minimal collateral damage."

Sage scowled.

Natalie smiled a smug grin. "What's the matter, Sage? Worried about something?"

"Just wanted to make sure people would be safe and everything," Sage said.

"That's really good of you. Makes sense why you're a nurse. We'll be really careful. People will only get hurt if they refuse to cooperate, alright?"

Sage didn't respond.

There was no one else on the landing platform. The three of them got out without speaking a word. Dune kept his rifle slung over his shoulder, his suppressed shotgun in his hands. Clive had adorned himself in his usual suit and tie, with some light armor under the suit providing a little protection.

"Fashion and function," he said before he put on his helmet.

Natalie rolled her eyes.

The three of them moved in unspoken synchronization as Sage got into the driver's seat and took off into the air. Dune took point with the shotgun, Natalie stayed just behind him, and Clive brought up the rear, all with weapons ready. The Theta protocol sirens had gone silent when the Vanguardsman had been captured and the city seemed colorless now, devoid of the flashing red lights and noise as people either escaped into their Creator contacts or hid in the depths of their homes.

"You know, she could just leave without us," Dune muttered quietly when they reached a corner.

"The skycar won't let her," Clive said. "If she goes further than twenty miles from the city, the SmartDrive protocol I put into the system will ground her."

Effective, Natalie thought. *Wonder if that's what he was programming while we were flying.*

Dune nodded, then moved up to the entrance. He and Natalie stood watch, weapons ready as Clive hunched over and began hacking the door. He tapped his wrist once, then pulled out a few small, metal tools that helped him pry off the panel covering the door's automated system. He had his mobile interface plugged in almost immediately.

Syndicate Weapons Cache 24168 had an interesting floorplan, from what Natalie had seen in Clive's files. It was, effectively, a concrete box within a small concrete building. The box sat in the center of one large room about the size of an average Seattle apartment. The cache itself was the size of a nice living room with one entrance, which was blocked by a heavy, metal door.

Clive looked at his wrist and a small watch lit up on the surface of his protective gauntlets. With a few clicks, they were in.

Ten soldiers stood on the other side, surrounding the cache. The Syndicate military crest was stamped onto their breastplates. As assumed, the Syndicate didn't guard their big guns with people from the City Guard.

The soldiers were quick. They raised their weapons, ducking behind metal barricades that rose out of the concrete floor.

Natalie and Dune were quicker. They ducked behind the cover of the doorway and opened fire. Two of the guards went down immediately, taken off their feet by Dune's shotgun rounds. Nat felled two more, one bullet going through the first's visor and another punching through a weak spot in the armor protecting the other's neck. In an instant, the blank gray concrete of the room was splattered with red and pink. Years ago, she would've squirmed inside, but she was an adult, now. She'd learned to deal with killing people.

With another click on Clive's watch, the metal barricades disappeared, receding back into the floor. The soldiers had no chance, no cover. Natalie killed four more of them. Dune only got two.

Clive was already at the box's door, plugging in. Natalie was right there with him. She pressed herself against the doorway, letting her assault rifle hang from her by its strap while she drew her SMG. It'd be more effective in the tight space.

Dune pressed against the other side of the doorway, shotgun in hand. "This is reckless, Nat. There's no way this goes well for us."

"Shut up and let's save the world," Natalie said. "Weapons ready."

"You'll want to get a grenade out, Douglas," Clive said, still tapping away.

"Won't that wreck the Harnesses?" Dune said.

"Nah, they're kept in sturdy containers," Clive said. "I checked the security feed while we were on our way here. There's one active Harness in there. Big Black Class with a strength Ability. That's what you're gonna blow up."

Convenient, Natalie thought.

Dune frowned, unclipped a grenade from his bandolier and pulled the pin. "A grenade will do it?"

Clive shrugged. "Probably. Either way, door's opening."

Natalie frowned. *Seems like he's got less of a plan than he let on.*

The door slid open with the sound of hydraulics before she could think too much about it. There, right on the other side of the door, stood an eight-foot-tall mountain of black metal and blood-red light.

Oh, good, Natalie thought.

She narrowly avoided a fist that moved with the speed and force of a skycar. The huge, black appendage slammed into the wall she'd been leaning against a heartbeat before.

"We're hosed!" Dune yelled, falling back.

Shut up and shoot, Natalie thought. She also fell back, spraying the Harness's visor with her suddenly-insignificant SMG. Grenades were the only thing they had that might do some damage to the thing, but they'd all get roasted in the blast with the Harness this close.

"Stand down!" the Harness said. The big thing's voice was a rough, digital roar

With a touch of the watch, Clive closed the door. Thick metal slammed into the Harness hard enough to stop it in its tracks, but not quite strong enough to sever anything. It caught the mechanical armor in the neck, slamming it into the wall. Only the large head and arm of the black, eerily-glowing machine remained on their side. The huge arm flailed, lashing out at Clive as the Harness attempted to heave the door open with its other hand. The war machine took the old man in the chest.

Natalie grimaced. *That's not good.*

Dune, not missing a beat, tossed his grenade. The small black ball rolled under their attacker. A second went by, during which the Harness desperately scrambled and pushed against the door, nearly managing to get it open, trying to bend its over-large arm to knock the explosive away. Natalie watched, crouched low, ready to move at a moment's notice. Then, with a blast of light and a burst of force, the grenade detonated.

Come on, Natalie thought.

The Harness's knees buckled. Natalie unclipped a grenade and Dune unclipped another of his own. Two more blasts shook the room, bringing the Harness to its knees.

"Stand down!" the Harness roared. "Reinforcements are inbound. Whether you manage to disable this armor or not, you will be apprehended."

Natalie removed the next grenade's pin, then waited.

One, two, three, she thought.

"Cooperate immediately," the Harness said.

Four, five, she thought. Then she threw the grenade like a baseball. Just as the grenade was about to bean the Harness in the visor, it exploded, rocking the wrecked pile of armor and power. The blood-red lights fizzled and sputtered and the mass of metal went still.

Natalie made a beeline to Clive. The old man was laying, sprawled out, on the concrete amidst the bodies of the guards. One of his arms was bent the wrong way and the light armor he'd worn under his suit was seriously dented.

"It appears that I got blood on my suit," he coughed.

Idiot, Natalie thought. She began patting the older man down, Dune standing right behind her, rifle in hand. "Do you have any botshots?" she said.

"Right breast pocket," Clive said.

She reached in, finding three of the thick, pen-length metal cylinders. Removing the cap revealed three thick, sharp needles.

"Nice stuff," Dune said.

"This will hurt for a second," Natalie said.

"Oh no," Clive said. "I'm already so comfortable, though."

Dune huffed. "Insufferable even when he's dying."

Clive gave a weak smile. "You know it, Douglas."

"Both of you, shut up," Natalie said. She stuck one of the needles into the informant's decimated arm and the silvery solution within shot into Clive's flesh with a hiss of pressurized air. The informant grunted, wincing.

"I'm going to need to take off the vest you're wearing," Natalie said.

"Sounds excellent," Clive said. "That'll hurt a lot, but it's no big deal. I'm tough in addition to dashing and intelligent."

Natalie rolled her eyes. "How do I take it off?" she said.

"It's voice activated," Clive said. Then, slightly louder, "New Suit: detach."

A few automated latches unclasped, revealing a little of Clive's torso. The bruising was already setting in, and his ribs looked misshapen. Despite obvious attempts to conceal his pain, Natalie could see the older man's ribs weren't where they ought to be. She administered the second injection quickly.

Clive's arm was already moving, slowly, back into its natural position. Nanites rushed through his veins, eventually reaching the broken bones and torn tissue, sewing them together and releasing anesthetic at pre-programmed intervals. His face was strained, his jaw clamped, but he was starting to relax. His good hand eased out of a fist.

"You good?" Natalie said.

"Good enough," Clive said. "Give me the third one in the ribs. Some are still busted."

Natalie nodded, gave the man the third injection, then stood. "We've got to move."

Clive nodded. "Yeah, I think the nanites have me put back together enough."

Dune helped him up.

"Thank you, Douglas," Clive said.

"Seriously, man, call me Dune. Please."

"Sure, sure," Clive said, walking back to the box's doorway. He carefully clambered onto the immobile husk of a Harness, periodically grunting or hissing with pain. "Keep up, kids, we've still got work to do."

Dune rolled his eyes. "He's insane."

"Yes," Natalie said. "Insane and getting us Harnesses. Come on."

She climbed over the Harness quickly. She figured the pilot was still alive, inside. She wondered what it was like, being trapped inside that much armor. Probably dark.

She squeezed through the mostly-closed hydraulic door before she got a view of the cache's interior. The concrete box was much more interesting on the inside than on the outside. A single light shone down from the center of the ceiling, illuminating the Harnesses that lined the walls. Each were stored standing in thick, glass containers, their helmets and breastplates open to allow the pilots to climb into their powerful shells. There was another big, large Harness, likely one of the ones with super strength, but most were just slightly larger than their pilot would be.

Clive was already at the console in the middle of the room, flipping through different displays. He tapped, typed, and swiped until three of the containers slid open.

Clive removed his helmet and looked to Natalie. He smiled, a crazy look in his eye, his clothes still stained with blood.

"After you, m'lady," he said, pointing at one of the Harnesses.

A rush went through Natalie's veins and a small, unconscious smile sprung onto her lips. She climbed into the black, metal shell, letting it close in around her.

For a second, she stood, unmoved, in the pitch-black interior of the armor. Something pricked her in the arm. Wires shifted around her and she felt a tingling at the base of her neck.

"Harness Connect online," said a beautiful, disembodied voice.

Natalie smiled.

.

11

Dune

Dune braced his extra-large Harness against the walls of their transport hold, stabilizing himself against the sudden turns and changes in speed. The ship's red lights and the blood-red light that emitted from his Harness were his only illumination. Clive was in the skyship's driver's seat since his Harness was only a little larger than the average person. Dune's was a solid nine feet tall, he hadn't fit so easily into this standard-sized prison transport.

Who knows how big Nat's is, he thought. *Small enough to be in the passenger's seat, I guess.*

As soon as her Harness had activated, she'd vanished. They'd tried communicating via hearlink, but her links had gone offline. Clive said something about it, Dune was sure, but he hadn't understood. The informant always had been a motor mouth and the whole super-speed Harness had only made it worse.

"Brcyrslf," Clive said over the intercom. They took a sharp turn, then shot forward faster than before.

At least we can see the stuff Nat touches, Dune thought. The seatbelt attached to the passenger's seat hadn't just buckled itself, they assumed.

Please let it have been Nat, Dune thought from within his Harness.

"You should really let Nat drive, Clive," he said through his hearlink.

"ScrwyDn," Clive said.

"Can't understand you, man," Dune said.

"Have you guys caught up with the transport yet?" Sage said through the hearlink.

"Not yet," Dune said. "Though Clive's definitely doing his best to catch up."

"All right, I'm ready to pick up," Sage said.

"You're doing really well for never having done this before," Dune said.

"Well thanks," Sage said. "I suppose that's some small consolation for being strong-armed into this."

"I'm glad," Dune said. His voice was almost drowned out by Clive's rapid, repeated knocks on the front of the hold.

"What's that?" Sage said.

"That's the signal," Dune said. Butterflies fluttered in his stomach as he approached the hold's door. Only then did he realize there was no handle on the door's interior.

Makes sense, he thought. *Don't want criminals letting themselves out.*

"There's no way to open the door," he said.

"You can run through buildings in that suit, right?" Sage said. "Who cares if there's a door?"

"Fair enough," he said.

He punched through the sturdy metal surface, which felt more like soggy cardboard beneath his blows.

Easier than I expected, he thought. *Scary easy.*

He peeled the metal back like it was the skin of an orange, welcoming the night wind into the skycar's hold. The Harness's exterior microphones let him hear it howl around him, though he couldn't feel its chill.

Surreal, Dune thought.

An imposing, black transport flew along a few dozen yards below them, its various angles and weapons illuminated by the moon's weak light. The huge vehicle looked like some great mechanical whale swimming through the night sky.

"You know," Dune said, looking at his target far below. "I'm actually afraid of heights."

"Qtwhnng," Clive said through the hearlink. He jolted their ride once again and, before Dune could do a thing about it, his Harness was falling into the thin embrace of the night sky.

"Screw you, Clive!" Dune yelled. Adrenaline coursed through his veins as he fell, tumbling through the air. He screamed as he hurtled through the night sky.

"Ggtmtgr," Clive replied.

Dune slammed into the jagged, metal surface, the transport's momentum causing him to skid across the ridge-filled surface, shooting sparks into the darkness. Dune struggled to grasp a handhold or foothold with his huge appendages as he tumbled along. His curses mixed with the sparks in the open air until he, thankfully, latched onto the transport's rear gun.

"I'll need to talk to a shrink until the day I die," Dune said. He climbed along the top of the flying vehicle.

"ShtpDnndgtsnsd," Clive said.

"Still can't understand you," Dune said. He dug his Harness's thick, powerful fingers into the top of the transport's surface. His fist repeatedly pounded at the skyship's steel. An explosion rocked him, nearly knocking him out of place. He toggled to the Harness's rear camera feed. The ship's topside turret was firing at him. Another shell hit his armor. He didn't stop. His fist slammed downward again and again, shells sparking as they ricocheted off his armor until, eventually, his fist punched through the metal plating.

Finally, he thought. Another shell rocked his Harness.

Then two Harnesses peeled back the metal surrounding Dune's newly-made hole, emerging from the chasm, their blue and red lights painting the sky like patriotic fireworks. One of them was larger, its armor dominated by the blood red light. The other was smaller, its arms and legs detailed with light the color of a blue sky.

Ah, hell, Dune thought. *Blue for flight, red for strength.*

Harness warfare was something of an interesting art. Dune had studied it a bit over the years, watching any tapes or vids he could get of Harnessed soldiers in action. All Black Class Harnesses were equipped with firearms and, on a few occasions, with laser cannons like the larger, but generally weaker, Silver Class Harnesses. These firearms were used against most Vanguardsmen and on the extremely rare and always dangerous renegade Harness. However, when super strength and durability came into play, the game changed. Skin that can deflect bullets will likely still have a hard time handling fists that hit like freight trains. So, Dune – dressed in a large, strength-enhancing Harness – found it to be no surprise that he was barraged by fists and feet. However, he did find it seriously dangerous. His Harness's huge, metal fingers lost a little more of their grip on the skyship's surface with each blow.

"I could really use some back up, Clive!" he yelled. Keeping a solid grip on the transport, he kicked the larger Harness, managing to knock it back for a few seconds. He swung at the smaller one, too, but it was faster, more nimble, and it flew gracefully out of his reach.

"MvDn!" Clive said.

"What?" Dune said.

"MOVE!" Clive said.

Dune launched himself forward with both arms, skidding across the top of the transport as the skyship with Clive at the controls bore down on the larger vehicle. The informant opened the driver's side door and bailed just before the vehicle rammed into the bigger Harness, smashing it into the top of the skyship. The prison transport crumpled with the impact, then was blown, scraping and squealing, off of the larger skyship and into the night.

"Nice job speaking coherently," Dune said, scanning the top of the skyship for any sign of Natalie.

"Thnkststlntfmn," Clive said. He latched onto the top of the hovership, struggling to hang on in spite of the whipping winds.

"Still a work in progress," Dune said, crawling toward the man as he spoke. "Where's Natalie?"

"Shsfn. Wgttgtnsd," Clive said, his grip slipping.

Dune picked up the informant in one of his Harness's huge arms. As far as he could see, there was no sign of Natalie.

"If she just fell to her death, I'm gonna kill you, man," Dune said. "That's a promise."

"Dntbdrmtc," Clive said. "Shsfn."

Dune cradled the hacker in one of his arms and glanced around them. The bigger Harness wasn't moving, at the moment, its frame crushed into the top of the transport. The smaller one had retreated to a safe distance and seemed to be lining up a shot on Clive.

No you don't, Dune thought. He lowered the informant into the skyship's interior. If Nat was dead, he'd kill Clive himself. No Harness would take that right from Dune.

Clive raced off in the blink of an eye while Dune scanned the transport's topside, looking for any indication of his sister. He saw nothing.

"Great," he said. *This all gives me a headache.*

He climbed into the transport. "She probably fell off the transport. For all I know, she didn't even make it out of the skycar."

The ship's interior was demolished. Holes had been punched through the walls, dents lined every available flat surface, and a few broken Harnesses littered the place. In the middle of it all stood the Vanguardsman, his black, crystalline armor glinting in the flickering, fluorescent light. Clive was at his side, animatedly gesturing and speaking absolute nonsense as he dodged the Vanguardsman's blows. The two of them danced around the room, Moore lashing out and carefully jabbing while Clive nimbly dipped and ducked.

How'd Moore get out? Dune thought.

He didn't get to think about it for long. The two Harnesses with red and blue light flew through the hole Dune had just created. The bigger one was sparking with one of its arms hanging at an odd angle, but apparently getting hit with a transport hadn't been enough to finish it. Dune turned to face the oncoming assault of black armor and light, Clay and Clive freezing mid-fight to see the oncoming enemies.

Dune took a deep breath and lunged forward. He sent the big one flying into the opposite wall with a right-handed jab. The smaller one dodged his second swing, sending Dune stumbling across the floor. *Dumb armor's top heavy,* he thought. Then the Harness planted a solid two-footed kick between his shoulder blades.

He soared through the air, head over heels, eventually colliding face-first with the same wall he'd knocked the bigger Harness into. The big guy backhanded him with his one good arm, pounding Dune deeper into the metal wall. Another punch to the back pushed him further into the ship's steel frame, the metal wall screeching as it bent. He tried to get free, but the blows kept coming. He could feel the Harness straining around him, bending a little with each blow.

I'm going to die in this thing, Dune thought. *What's it like to die in a Harness? It's gotta be painful, all those pieces of metal pushing in on you.* He struggled, but another blow kept his Harness from getting free. He imagined what it would be like to have your spine broken and insides speared with pieces of your own battle armor.

You're going to die, he thought. *You let your dad die. You watched your mom die. Kent died saving you. Now your sister's probably fallen to her death, or something, and you're just going to lay down and die too.* Anxiety seized his chest, making it hard to breathe. *You've done nothing to save any of them, and now you're too weak to save yourself.*

In desperation, he lashed out with one of his feet, barely managing to connect with something. He pushed against the twisted, bending metal that surrounded him, managing to get one arm and part of his torso free, just enough for him to see the Harness's next hit before it landed, catching it with his free hand.

"I'm not dying today, buddy," he said.

Adrenaline roared through his veins. He pulled the Harness in close and dealt a solid headbutt to its helmet, dropping it to the ground. It tried to strike with its other arm, but it was still bent out of shape from colliding with the transport. Dune, meanwhile, pulled his other arm free and dealt a solid hammerfist to the top of its helmet, driving it down into the Harness's shoulders and pushing the Harness further into the floor beneath them. Then, with a heave, Dune pulled his leg free of the wall and kicked the Harness onto its back.

Let's see how you like it, he thought, stomping the Harness into the floor. The metal bent around it, beginning to trap the armor within the skyship's shell. *Trapped, powerless. Scared.*

He knelt down on the Harness's shoulders, keeping it from moving its arms. He could see Clay and Clive moving in his peripheral vision, but he ignored them, raining blows down on the Harness's helmet, pushing it deeper and deeper into the skyship. The helmet came a little more undone with each blow, gears and pieces of metal flying off, the armor dissolving underneath him.

Then there was blood. He dealt a blow and blood splattered, spraying through some opening in the decimated suit of armor. The sight of it jolted Dune back to reality, back to the aches and pains and the sound of chaos. He realized he'd been crying.

"GtnyrftDn! Wvstllgtstfftd," Clive said.

Dune stood slowly, his Harness making hair-raising squeals as he did, bent steel scraping against armor plates. "Sorry about that," he whispered to the dead soldier within the Harness beneath him. Blood dripped from his Harness's hands.

He turned and surveyed the room. The smaller Harness was on the ground, unmoving. Clay and Clive simply stood, watching him.

"What?" Dune said.

Moore eyed him warily. "I don't know you, but you seem like someone who could use a break."

Dune huffed. "Don't even know what a break is, anymore."

"Tllmbtt," Clive said.

"That's not good," Moore said.

"Trust me, buddy, I know," Dune said. "Now, onto more important topics, where is my sister?"

"You have a sister?" Moore said.

"The Angel? You fangirled over her earlier today," Dune said.

"Oh, you're the two who were with her in the sewer today?" Clay said.

"Yessir," Dune said. "I'm her brother, Dune."

"Bnkrlllfthrvglntffrts," Clive said. "Nbgdl."

"Do you know what he's saying?" Moore said.

"No clue," Dune said. "Let's get to the cockpit."

They moved through the skyship's halls, working their way up to the front of the ship, with Clive and Clay walking in front of him. The Vanguardsman's dark, reflective armor glinted in the light of Dune's and Clive's Harnesses. He carried a rifle, which seemed unnecessary, to Dune. The guy could hit much harder than a bullet. Dune, meanwhile, had to keep his Harness hunched over to make it through the ship's inner workings, squeezing around corners and turns, but he managed to get through. Periodically, Clive would vibrate and jolt, as if he were about to take off in a flash.

"So, Dune's not a very normal name," Clay said.

Dune shrugged his Harness's large shoulders. "It's what people call me."

"Tsdmbnm. HsrllynmdDgls," Clive said.

"And that guy?" Clay said.

"The Harness talking gibberish is Clive de Santos, our informant and sponsor," Dune said.

"Pretty hands-on informant," Clay said.

"He says he likes to see the fruit of his labors," Dune said. "Though it's more the fruit of our labors."

Clay motioned for them to hold at the next corner, crouching to look at something on the ground.

"What is it?" Dune said.

"Explosive trap."

"How do you know?"

"All skyships of this model have an explosive hooked up to a sensor right before you reach the cockpit," Clay said. "It stays online, even once the ship's main batteries fail. Uses a reserve battery. The sensor knows if you don't have a Syndicate uniform or armor on." He pulled the floor panel up, revealing the mechanism beneath. He turned to Clive. "You're going to need to pull those wires before the motion sensor can trip the explosive. Dune and I will be fine, either way, but the blast will damage you pretty good."

Clive shook his head so fast his Harness's head blurred.

"Is he saying no?" Clay said.

"Hell if I know," Dune said.

Clive began tapping a metal panel on the wall, his fingers battering the panel until it dented, then started bending away. His Harness's yellow light glowed brighter the faster he went. The man in the hyper-fast Harness bent the panel backward before Clay or Dune could say a thing. With a flash of light, he tore up the wiring on the other side. For a second, Dune waited for an explosion to tear through the hall.

Nothing happened.

"Well done," Dune said.

"Mmrthnprttyfc," Clive said. The guy kept working, reaching under the floor panel Clay had peeled open. In seconds, he had the explosives out of the floor and strapped, with new wiring, to the wall.

"What does that do?" Clay said.

"I'm sorry, this may seem repetitive, but I don't know," Dune said.

"Ltsgfrnds," Clive said, then he bolted down the hallway.

"Guess it's time to go," Dune said.

"Guess so," Clay said.

They pressed down the hallway to the cockpit. When they reached it, they found bodies littering the floor. Some were bleeding, all were adorned in Syndicate uniform. Some of the wall's panels were punctured with a few bullet holes and the door was hanging off its hinges.

The pilot's chair swiveled around, Natalie resting comfortably inside, her skin devoid of a single scratch.

Oh, thank goodness, Dune thought. *Miracles still happen.* The tightness in his chest eased up a little. Not entirely, of course. They were still flying in a seriously damaged Syndicate skyship, after all.

"That suit was useful, but I don't think I'll wear it much," Natalie said. She gestured at the empty metal shell in the corner. "You almost ran me over a few times."

"Mr. Moore, this is my sister, Natalie," Dune said. "I guess she's our pilot today."

"And the reason why my restraints released me, I'm guessing," Clay said.

Natalie smiled. "Freed you on my way to the cockpit. It's a wonder what you can do when you're invisible."

"So I've heard," Clay said.

From who? Dune thought. *Do Vanguardsmen just talk about this stuff whenever they're together?*

"About to put her down," Natalie continued. The skyship slowed itself and began to descend. "We've got another transport ready on the ground. You got anywhere to be, Clay?"

"Actually, I do," he said. "How capable is the skyship we'll be leaving in?"

That was when they heard the squealing sound of metal piercing through metal and a sickening, hollow sound. Dune turned to face it, then grimaced, fists clenching.

Clive fell to his knees, the tip of a bayonet jutting out of the older man's Harness. Blood dripped from the blade's tip, landing on his thighs, then trickling down to the floor. He fell, limp, onto his side, his attacker nowhere to be seen.

The room was silent besides Clive's coughing, struggling breaths. *Can't help him yet,* Dune thought. *Threat's still in the room.*

His eyes immediately darted to where Natalie's Harness had been only seconds ago. Maybe Natalie hadn't killed one of the Syndicate officers in the cockpit? Maybe one had only been wounded and managed to get the battle armor on? But no, it was still there in the corner, limp and unused.

All Dune could see was a dying man.

12

Clay

"Brace yourselves for a dive!" Natalie yelled.

Clay leaped toward Clive's body, his obsidian forming around him as the ship went into a dive. He reached the bleeding man just as the skyship's momentum started propelling them up and out the cockpit's door. Dune, meanwhile, braced his hands against the ceiling, trying to use the suit of armor to form a metal wall between his sister and the rest of the room. Clay pushed off the cockpit door, managing to secure Clive into one of the other seats in the cockpit.

A few feet behind him, something thudded into the ceiling.

There they are, Clay thought.

He moved fast, pushing himself off Clive's seat and launching toward the sound. The skyship was at cruising altitude, so he had some time to dispatch the attacker, but not much at their rate of descent.

Probably only a few seconds.

He collided with something he couldn't see, wrapped his arms around it as they tumbled through the air. While most Harnesses would crumple in his tight embrace, this invisible armor held strong.

Strength and stealth, he thought. *This may a minute.*

Then an invisible force slammed into his crotch. Thankfully, his obsidian took most of the blow, but some of the shock struck home.

Definitely going to take a minute, Clay thought, hunching to avoid any future strikes. The two of them tumbled through the air, flying back toward the cockpit's door. The skyship, propelled downward by the Angel – Natalie was her name — was hurtling toward the earth,

98

faster and faster. Clay pounded the Harness again and again. After a few blows, he felt the metal start to give way. Eventually, he punched through the metal casing, a sharp crack shooting through the cockpit's turmoil as his opponent's ribs snapped. The invisible assassin grunted with pain, unsuccessfully struggling to counteract Clay's brutal attacks. Eventually, Clay dented the armor enough to pry the metal casing open, tearing apart the wires and mechanisms concealed within until the battered Harness flickered into view.

The Harness, in desperation, began striking harder than it had before. Clay took an extraordinarily powerful elbow to the chin. Then, while he was still off balance, the Harness grabbed him by the head and slammed its armored knee into the obsidian coating his head. The blow sent him flying back into the ceiling. He caught himself on a light fixture just in time to defend himself from a flying kick before it connected.

"Bye, bud," Clay said. Then he threw the Harness down the hall. The soldier managed to catch the doorway, but Clay wasn't done. He launched himself off of the light fixture, then kicked the Harness square in the chest with both feet. The soldier shot down the hall, setting off the explosive's motion sensor, decimating the already damaged Harness.

Guess that's what the fast guy was doing, Clay thought. *Hope it doesn't hurt the ship or anything.*

"Pull up!" he yelled in the direction of the cockpit.

Natalie pulled at the skyship's controls, flipping a multitude of switches and swiping across numerous touchscreens. The skyship began to right itself, but it was pulling out of the dive too slowly.

"Nat, pull up!" Dune said.

"The hoverdrive's not calibrating!" Nat said. Her hands rapidly danced around the ship's controls. "Forward thrusters can't overpower our trajectory!"

"Get to the point!" Clay said. He launched himself to the seat Clive's limp body was strapped into, placing himself between the older man and the ship's viewport just in case.

"Brace for impact!" Natalie said. The abandoned ruins of Seattle's suburbs grew more and more defined on the other side of the cockpit's viewport.

Clay grimaced. He covered the downed man's body as best he could, wrapping himself around the Harness and the chair. He could still be alive inside that metal shell, for all he knew. They were just feet from the city's rooftops now, so close Clay could almost see individual leaves on the trees below. Dune, still inside his Harness, protectively wrapped as much of the armored suit as he could around his sister.

Then they made contact.

Clay felt the skyship plow through the first few buildings without too much trouble. He heard something punch through the viewport and saw a metal beam spearing through the shoulder mechanism of Dune's Harness out of the corner of his eye. Masses of dust and debris billowed into the cockpit. Clay took a large chunk of something hard to the back but managed to maintain his obsidian, concrete crumbling around him. Then the ship caught something, bringing it to an abrupt halt and launching Clay past the others and out of the viewport. He didn't know what had happened until he was soaring through the air, Clive and the chair still in his arms.

This is going to hurt, he thought.

The sounds of wind and wreckage assaulted his ears even through the protection of his obsidian. There was another, smaller eruption of shattered concrete and wood as he burst through a few walls, haphazardly flipping through the sky until he, too, crashed into the earth, bouncing and tumbling along.

He already felt the sharp pain of bruised bones echoing throughout his body. It was the kind of pain that lingered, pulsing in time with the in and out of his breathing. He was slow to stand, his obsidian coated in scratches and cracks.

Clive was in far worse condition. Clay scowled as he looked at the battered Harness that housed the old man's body, still strapped into the now-deformed chair. The suit of armor was thoroughly dented, marred by the walls and debris through which they had tumbled. Dried blood painted some of the black armor a rusty, dead color while blood still flowed out of other crevices, glistening in the night's dim light. Clay pried the Harness out of the seat, then pried the Harness off the man, progressively revealing a blood-soaked suit and tie and a well-kept mane of gelled, graying hair.

Not a very practical outfit, he thought.

He checked the man's pulse, hoping against the odds that there would still be a heartbeat. The old man's body was still as the grave.

Clay sighed. *Can't blame a guy for hoping.*

A quiet beeping disturbed the night, growing louder and louder as he tore the armor open, piece by piece. Hidden in the midst of the blood and battered fabric, an unnatural, bright gold light shone, lighting Clive's immobile visage.

"Come on, man," Clay muttered. "You're already dead. Please tell me you didn't rig your body to blow."

Still adorned in his scuffed obsidian, Clay carefully prodded the dead man's bloody clothes, peeking into the depths of the soiled, battered suit and gently feeling around the stained, bloody expanse of the not-so-white shirt. After a few tense moments, he withdrew his right hand, a small black cylinder resting in his palm. A single button was embedded in the smooth surface of the contraption, blinking gold in time with the gentle beeping that emanated from within.

"What've you got there?" a voice said from behind him.

Clay whirled to face the unknown questioner, fists clenched. Natalie stood alone amidst the rubble and ruin of the suburban wasteland.

"Easy," she said. "It's just me."

"Sorry," Clay said. "I'm used to people trying to kill me when they sneak up like that."

"I'll do my best not to surprise you, then," she said. "What've you got?"

Clay held up the black cylinder, the golden button blinking in the darkness. "Something your man Clive had on him when he died."

"He's dead?"

Clay nodded. "No pulse and lots of lost blood. Unless y'all carry bags of O-negative, defibrillators, and half a dozen botshots, he's gone."

Natalie nodded curtly, then looked at the cylinder. "Know what it does?"

"No idea," Clay said. He handed it to her. "Can't find out yet, either. A Syndicate skyship will be here any second."

"We've got a getaway car," she said.

"Is it a high-class cruiser?" Clay asked. "It'll need to be, if we're going to beat the ship they send."

"Alright, what's your plan?"

"Get ahold of your driver. We'll need to move on foot," Clay said.

"You sure we can get out of Seattle? A lot of bugs live in this city."

Clay shrugged. "Experience says we can make it out without getting infected and my gut says we'll have to."

"Sounds good to me," Natalie said. "I'm just going to need your help getting Dune out of his Harness first."

Clay smiled. "Sounds good."

They climbed over and through the wrecked buildings surrounding the skyship. The battered, immobile shell of a Harness hung out of the wrecked skyship's viewport as they approached, black and dark as the night. Clay, adorned in his obsidian, climbed up to the viewport and peeled the armor like an orange. The crash had softened it up significantly. There, in the center of the hulking metal cocoon, lay a bloodied and battered Dune.

"That hurt," Dune said, spitting out some blood.

Natalie's brow furrowed. "You're good, though. Right?"

Looks pretty bad to me, Clay thought.

Dune spat out some more blood. "Yeah, I'm fine. Just busted a lip, I think. Pretty hopped up on adrenaline, though. Probably in shock too."

Almost imperceptibly, Clay saw Natalie relax. It was a bittersweet moment for him. Another family saved for another day, only to remind him of all the family he'd lost.

Life goes on, he thought. He reached his hand down into the contorted metal. "Let me help you out of there, man." Dune took the hand and, after some finagling, all three stood side by side.

"We need to leave now," Clay said.

"What about calling our ride?" Natalie asked.

"Well yeah, call your driver, but don't tell them to meet us here. Tell them to meet us a mile or two north of here. Otherwise, we'll all just get busted together."

"Makes sense to me," Dune said. He looked around. "Where's Clive?"

"Dead," Natalie said. She handed Dune one of the rifles she was carrying. "Let's go. I'll make the call while we walk."

They left the wreckage behind and began to wind their way through the abandoned suburbs. Natalie put the call through, giving orders to their driver in hushed tones.

Guess she's the one in charge, Clay thought.

Clay couldn't get a good view of Dune's face in the darkness, but his hunched shoulders and silence cast a somber feeling over the man. Eventually, he spoke up.

"Clive's dead?" Dune asked.

"Yeah," Clay said. "I did what I could, but he's dead."

"Man. He actually died."

"Yep. Hard stuff."

"Yeah, yeah. Honestly, the guy got on my nerves. He was a condescending prick constantly strong-arming me and flashing his expensive stuff." Dune crossed himself. "Don't want to speak evil of the dead or anything. Nat was really tight with him. He believed in her and pushed her to do what she wanted, even when I was talking her out of it. Especially when I was talking her out of it."

"So, you're not the hugest fan of the Angel stuff, then?" Clay said.

"You probably think I'm selfish. She does some good and helps people out when she can. Broke up some gangs, took down a sex trafficking ring, stuff I guess you already heard about. I'm just the big brother, I guess. Supposed to keep her alive, you know?" He glanced at Natalie, who was ending her call. "She doesn't care much what I think though."

"Our ride's going to land a mile north of us," Natalie said. If she'd heard what Dune had said, she didn't acknowledge it.

"You see what I mean," Dune said.

"Yep," Clay said. *He's surprisingly ready to share family drama with a stranger,* he thought. "Either of you mind letting me use your hearlinks? I'm going to put a call through to my team, who should be able to get us out of here."

"Should be?" Dune said.

"Should be."

"That's not entirely comforting."

"Come on, Dune. Just give him the hearlinks," Natalie said.

"Fine. I'd just rather not have Sage ditch our prepared ride out of here if our only other shot at a flight out of Seattle is a maybe," Dune said, handing the hearlinks to Clay.

"We'll be fine," Natalie said. "We walked across Washington once. We can do it again, if we have to."

"Y'all, we aren't walking across Washinton," Clay said. "They'll come."

Dune grumbled something in response, but Clay couldn't hear. The call was already going through.

By the call's sixth buzz, Clay was nervous. Protocol dictated radio response in a maximum of three seconds. Relief washed over him once they finally did pick up.

"Verification, please," Chik said. Her voice was hollow and quiet, the way it always was when she was anxious.

"Four zero five, Michigan Alabama Swaziland," Clay said. "It's me."

He heard Chik let out an exasperated breath on the other end. "You'd better not be compromising the emergency frequency, Moore," she said.

"Of course not," Clay answered. "You guys en route to the prison? Have you got time for a stop just outside of Seattle?"

"Did you bust out, Clay?" he heard Ice ask in the background. "How'd you bust out?"

"No way," May said. "It's a trap or something."

"It's not a trap," Clay said. "I didn't really bust out, I was busted out more than anything else. Speaking of which, there are three people I need extracted with me."

"None of them are bugged or tracked, are they?" May asked.

"I don't have a scanner, May, I just got out of jail," Clay said. "I'll be shocked if they do have tracers, but y'all can check them when you pick us up."

"I'm using this call to triangulate your location," Ice said. "I'm betting we'll arrive in an hour."

Clay frowned as he glanced at the sky. "We may be caught before then."

Dune gave him a concerned look.

"Shouldn't have gotten caught in the first place," May said.

"I love how much you care," Clay said. "I guess we'll keep moving and hope we don't get killed. We'll call in an hour so you can track our position."

"All right, that'll work well enough," Chik said.

"Fantastic," Clay said.

"J.J. wants to talk to you," Chik said.

Clay tensed up immediately. "Uh oh, looks like I've got to go. Bye." He hung up before Chik could say anything.

Don't want to have that talk yet, he thought. His stomach was already turning with anxiety. *J won't pull punches after this stunt.*

"How soon until they arrive?" Dune asked.

"One hour," Clay said.

"Yeah, that's too long."

"Oh, come on," Natalie said. "We can hold it together for an hour."

"Nat, Clive just died," Dune said. "We're one man down. You think we can get through the next hour without losing someone else?"

"No one's dying," Clay said. "We stay on the ground, stay hidden, and keep quiet. We'll live."

Dune huffed. A skyship hummed somewhere above them, its headlight piercing the darkness.

"That your ride?" Clay said.

"Yeah," Nat seethed. "I thought I told her to keep her lights out."

"Well, she didn't," Clay said. Almost without thinking, he ran to the descending skyship, the misty rain running down the surface of his obsidian shell. Aged litter and debris clattered, his careless steps scattering the long-dormant ruins. He was there when the hum faded and the sleek, expensive-looking skyship landed. The headlights blazed into the night's darkness even once the ship had touched down.

The driver's side door opened, revealing the red-headed woman from the sewers, a pistol strapped to her hip. Clay reached across her and into the skyship's interior before she said a word, shutting off the lights. The woman leaned away from him reflexively.

"You do know I don't have the virus, right?" Clay said.

"Of course," she said defensively. "You were just kind of in my personal space and I don't know you at all."

"Sorry for invading your personal space," Clay said. He scanned the sky. A deeper hum sounded above them, signaling the arrival of a larger skyship.

"What's wrong?" the driver asked.

"You were followed," Clay said. "I'm afraid I'm going to have to carry you, now."

13

Clay made it back to the others in less than five seconds, bracing Sage's neck to prevent whiplash. She'd told him her name just before he'd picked her up.

Because stranger danger, he thought.

The others had hidden themselves in one of the nearby dilapidated houses. Clay only saw them once Dune shifted, the darkness was so thick. They were peering through a hole in the wall using the scope on one of the rifles. Dune handed Clay the rifle when he approached.

"Harnesses," Dune said quietly.

The black suits of armor roamed the suburban wasteland, clothed in an array of different colors. Clay could see three, in total. One had light blue shining from within its arms that arced and flowed, like a bluebird's wings, while the breastplate and legs blazed with orange light that roiled and churned like fire. The armor on the left, however, had lines of pure white and deep, regal purple that sometimes mixed and sometimes seemed to fight with one another. However, neither of these Harnesses captivated Clay's attention as much as the third. This armor radiated light that was blue as the most intense fire, red as crimson in other places, and had a facemask that burned yellow as the sun.

"McGrath's here," Clay said.

Dune nodded.

"The Chancellor of North America?" Sage said. With them so crammed around the wall's crevice, Clay could feel her breath on his neck.

"Yes, that McGrath," Clay said. He looked up from the rifle's scope at her huddled outline. "Sorry."

"Oh, no big deal," Sage said. "I guess I just didn't realize that you were important enough for them to send the guy in charge of the whole continent."

"Well, now you know," Clay said. "I'm one in a million."

"He's also humble," Dune mumbled as he stood.

"What are we going to do?" Sage said.

"We'll keep moving north-northeast," Clay said. "We'll need to stick to the houses more than we have so far and we'll need to be extremely careful, but we'll survive if we keep our heads."

Sage nodded, the motion looking like a particularly intense bout of shivering in the darkness. The others muttered their assent as well. Natalie stood first, tiptoeing into the darkness, then Clay and the others followed.

It'd be nice if we had some coats, Clay thought. He was still in his thin white prison clothes and Natalie and Dune were wearing some pretty light clothes, no doubt having left coats and armor behind to fit into their stolen Harnesses better. *Wouldn't be good to have anyone catching a chill. A stray cough at a bad time could kill us.*

Sage moved at his side with a calculated care, her feet almost silently traversing the asphalt, grass, and concrete, narrowly dodging treacherous pieces of rubble and glass that may have revealed her. She'd tied her shoulder-length hair back in a ponytail that quickly had devolved into what would more accurately be described as a wet, limp dog's tail. Even still, she didn't complain.

She's doing pretty good, he thought.

Clay realized how long he'd been living this kind of life as he watched Sage's movements and nervous, shifting stance. It'd been years since he'd spent a day without having to defend his life. When was the last time he'd passed an hour without feeling like he was in some kind of mortal danger? He tried to remember as he moved into the ruin of the nearest house.

I think it's been about a year, he realized. He smiled a cynical smile. *Good old Seattle. Keeping me on my toes.*

"The Harnesses are on the move," Natalie said. She'd managed to ascend the wrecked mess of the ruin's staircase. She perched at the top, like some fierce bird of prey. She moved slowly, watching the enemy through her rifle's scope.

Wonder how long it's been since she went a day without her gun,

Clay thought.

"They're scanning the skyship's cockpit," she said. "No sign that they know where we are, just yet."

"Then we keep our heading," Clay said.

"Wait," Natalie said abruptly. Clay saw Sage tense up out of the corner of his eye. *Easy,* he thought. *Easy.*

"They're leaving," Natalie said.

"Well, that's bad," Clay said. "We're leaving."

"What, why's that bad?" Sage said.

"Sage, you saw that video we showed you, right?" Dune said, loading his shotgun.

"Of course," she said.

"Video?" Clay said.

"It's a short vid of the Hart commanding bugs," Natalie said. Her face fell a little. "Clive found it."

"There's a vid of that?" Clay said. "Do y'all have it?"

"No, Clive had it uploaded back in his penthouse," Dune said. "My point is, if the Syndicate can call in hordes of Infected whenever they're needed, who will they use to search abandoned houses? Three Harnesses or three hundred Infected?"

Sage went stiff. Clay heard a faint hum, and turned around to find the skyship taking off into the sky.

"Let's move," he said.

They sprinted from house to house, crashing through flimsy weather-worn doors and bursting into desecrated living rooms and kitchens. The sound of their gasping populated the night's relative silence, their drenched footprints disrupted the stationary topography of yards that had not been touched in years.

Clay let his obsidian dissolve as they ran. While he didn't have a limited reserve of obsidian, his mental faculties could only maintain it for so long and he would obviously be needing it soon. Thorns and pebbles scraped his feet through the flimsy material of his standard-issue prison shoes while the misty rain quickly soaked him through.

They reached the overgrown forest, its trees and foliage overcoming any former confines or fences like a beast grown wild over the ages. Only then did Clay begin to hear the screeches.

"Move, Sage, move!" Dune yelled. Clay glanced over his shoulder to see her breathing heavily a few feet behind them.

The inhuman cries rose in volume, filling the air. Clay shot a look over his shoulder as he wove through trees, shrubs, and bushes of all sorts. He couldn't see any bugs yet, but their calls still sent adrenaline through his system.

The calls are coming from the direction of the land site, he thought. *We've just got to keep moving and we'll be able to reach a defensible position before they reach us.* Dune was still bellowing behind him, calling to Sage as she incrementally fell further behind.

Where'd Natalie go? Clay thought, checking to make sure they hadn't lost the young vigilante. After a few moments he found her, running a short distance in front of him.

Well, she's fine, he thought.

They erupted from the forest, a large, ghostly mansion rising amidst the overgrown grass in front of them, surrounded by a rusted fence.

This'll have to do, Clay thought, easily kicking in the front gates, no obsidian required.

Natalie darted ahead of him now, her rifle raised and at the ready. The screeches increased in volume, the cacophony piercing the otherwise-quiet night. They were at the house now, Natalie kicking down the front door. It caved in even easier than the gate, softened wood sabotaged by moss and rain. Natalie plunged inside while Clay waited at the doorway.

"Get in here," he hissed. He could hear Sage's ragged gasps before she reached the home, her lungs and diaphragm wracked by the force of her fear.

She's going to be a problem, he thought as she ran through the doorway. *We won't be able to hide too well if she's having a nervous breakdown.*

"Does this place have a basement?" Clay said. He barred the now-empty doorway with his body.

"Yeah, the stairs are right by the kitchen," Natalie said.

"The three of you get down there and hide," Clay said. "Find a corner in a room with no windows, if possible, and stay silent."

Sage nodded quietly, running downstairs as fast as she could. Natalie and Dune didn't follow suit, lingering by the stairs instead, guns in hand. Screeches were building up in a violent crescendo outside, the forest shifting with movement in the dark. The trees swayed as the mass of infected approached, pushed by a wave of flesh, bone, and corrupted blood.

"You sure you're good?" Natalie said.

"We'll see," Clay said. "McGrath may immediately engage once the horde finds us. If that's the case, we'll have to try and run. I can't take the guy; his Harness might be a bit too much for me."

"If he doesn't?" Dune said.

"We hold this position. I'll take ground floor, you two take positions on the second floor, try to thin out the herd for me before they get inside," Clay said.

"We don't have infinite ammo," Dune said. "I've only got four clips or so."

"Then make them count," Clay said. "You got any better ideas? Other plans?"

The two others shook their heads, though Clay could tell they were both frowning.

"Sounds like that's our play, then. Y'all have the time?"

"We've got forty minutes before your extraction crew reaches the area," Dune said.

"Beautiful," Clay said. "At least it's not an hour."

"It's not minute either," Dune said.

"You really seem like a cup half-empty kind of guy right now, Dune," Clay said. "If you've got a better idea, I'd love to hear it. Otherwise, please get downstairs and get ready."

Dune thudded down the stairs, grumbling as he went.

"Clay, I may have something," Natalie said. "There's that thing Clive had on him. Maybe it'd be useful."

"Well, give it a look," Clay said. "We'll need whatever help we can get."

Natalie got down on one knee, pulling the smooth, black cylinder from her backpack, its gold light still blinking.

"Think it might be a weapon?" Clay said.

"Doubt it, seems like something else," Natalie said, quietly. "If it is though, this is Clive we're talking about. It'd be some type of bomb." She pulled a small kit of screws and pointy pieces of metal from her bag. "Give me thirty seconds. I'll get it open, we'll check and see."

Someone thudded up the stairs and Dune appeared in the doorway to the basement. "What's going on?" he said.

"Nat's checking something Clive had," Clay said. "Could be useful."

"Can you do it downstairs?" Dune said to Nat.

The cylinder's casing popped open, revealing the inner workings of the device. "No," she said. "It'd be a mess to move, now that it's open."

"Nat, we've got to go," Dune said.

"Go then," Nat said.

Dune growled in frustration but didn't say anything else.

Clay looked down at Natalie, who had pulled a small, dim light from her bag to inspect the device. Her hands moved quickly as she carefully dissected Clive's mechanism, working with screws and tools as if they were scalpels and pincers.

"What've we got?" Clay said as the casing came apart.

"No idea," Natalie said, peering into the small device. "It's no bomb, though. No explosives to be found." She quickly reassembled the casing, her hands moving like united spiders. "Let's see what it does."

Screeches grew louder outside. Clay could almost make out the individual Infected moving through the trees nearby as he peeked through one of the kitchen windows.

"Make it quick," he said. "We're about to have company."

"Hold on," Natalie said. Her hands moved frantically, dancing faster and faster, exchanging one tool for another with every second. "I've got it."

"Hit the button," Clay said, still peering out the window, a rifle in each hand.

Natalie hesitated, took a deep breath, then pushed the blinking, gold button with her thumb.

A small flash of light emerged from within the cylinder, bright and gold just like the button. The light hung, suspended in the air for a moment, then coalesced into a singular form, that of a middle-aged woman in a plain, simple sun dress that reached her knees. Her short hair flowed slowly, as if she hung in zero gravity. She frowned once she opened her eyes, a graceful, small downturn of the lips, her intangible eyes filled to the brim with concern.

"Natalie, where's Clive?" the woman said.

"Um," Natalie said, glancing at Clay, unsure of what she should say. "He's dead. Who are you? Can you help us?"

The woman's jaw dropped and eyes went wide. "What's happening?"

"We're preparing to be attacked by a wave of Infected just outside Seattle," Clay said. "Do you do anything helpful?"

The woman shook her head. "No. Talk to me once this is over. I'm not much help outside of the quarantine zones."

Then, with a small blink of light, she disappeared back into the black cylinder.

Well, that did us no good, Clay thought. He tossed Natalie her rifle. "Get downstairs," he said.

Natalie nodded, shoving the odd cylinder into her backpack.

The horde moved through the forest outside like a river. It had taken a while to come, but now that it was here it swept the land, toppling small trees, avoiding the large ones. The screeching was constant now, a continuous wailing that tore through the passive night air and shook the walls of their shelter.

Not the biggest swarm I've seen, he thought, his mind flashing back to the horde that swept through Denver back when the Outbreak started.

A few of the bug-like people detached from the flow and approached the mansion, which was a hundred yards off-course from the flood of infected. They crept toward the house quietly, making small clicking and snapping noises with their stiff, jagged jaws. Clay hid in what remained of an old coat closet.

It'd be so nice if they searched the house and didn't find us, he thought. *If they'd just move on.*

The floorboards creaked in the front hall like old, lethargic creatures, too tired to protest the abuse. Even from his position down the hall, Clay could hear the creatures sniffing, air scraping against the stiff caverns of their nostrils. Their long, hard nails, grown out and neglected, dragged along the floorboards making a hollow scratching sound.

Leave, Clay thought through the scraping as the screeching began to grow a little quieter. *Leave with the others.*

The bugs, of course, did not listen to his inaudible pleas. They continued to sniff and smell, searching throughout the ruined ground floor's innards. Second after second, they drew incrementally closer to him and to the basement staircase, their breaths growing louder and louder, his blood flowing faster and faster through his veins.

Then someone bumped something downstairs. There was a thud that resounded throughout the mansion, followed by a muffled curse. The bugs, standing just feet from Clay's dilapidated coat closet, stopped in their tracks, their jagged breathing cut short.

Well, there goes that, Clay thought.

He didn't even bother to waste time opening the door. Clay burst straight through the piece of wood, splinters exploding outward as he, shrouded in obsidian, grabbed hold of the nearest bug. He threw the diseased creature up into the ceiling, where it securely lodged, managing to get only halfway through before it stopped amidst the mess of wood and nails. He slammed his fist into the chest of the next one, collapsing its rib cage and sending it flying into the hallway wall. The last two screeched in horror, scrambling over themselves to escape him. He was on them before they reached the door, punching holes through them with two quick blows.

He heard the screeches in the distance grow louder as the horde's hive mind relayed the mansion's location to each cranium. Already, he could envision their black eyes turning toward the secluded mansion, the black void of their massive pupils contrasting with their rice paper skin.

Clay sighed as the horde drew closer. How many minutes did they have left before extraction, now? Thirty-five minutes, maybe?

J.J., y'all can't get here fast enough, he thought. Resigned, he walked to the front door, staring out into the darkness at the amassing army of the diseased.

14

The night was torn apart by screams, screeches, squelches and the sound of shattering wood. The groaning house's bending wood sounded like a duet between an old cello and a gurgling bass and the screeches of the horde acted as tormented wind instruments. Clay, of course, added to the vocal performance. He stood in the mansion's doorway, swarmed by bugs, bellowing as he struck them down one after the other.

He fought with an absolute lack of restraint, attacking with all his might. He threw one Infected after another through the air, sending them soaring into the forest they had emerged from. His fists and feet flew right and left, effectively and efficiently killing the monstrosities. He tore out one of the decorative columns from the front porch, swinging the huge piece of wood like a baseball bat until it was a dissolving pulpy mess in his hands. Green blood flowed freely, puddling as the pale-skinned bodies piled all around him, the inhuman liquid coating Clay's obsidian armor.

This is going too well, Clay thought. *I'm going to wipe out the horde too fast. Then McGrath will show up and cart us off just before J.J. and the others get here.*

And yet, he couldn't let up. He had to keep the horde focused on him for the sake of the others.

He sent out a call, letting the hearlink buzz as he threw another infected into the crowd of its diseased compatriots, knocking a dozen or so of the deformed denizens off their feet and breaking the thrown bug's bones. Clay heard J.J. pick up the line as he clubbed another couple bugs with the porch's other pillar.

"What's your status?" J.J. said.

"We're caught by a horde of bugs," Clay said. Another swing of the pillar crushed five infected into the mud.

"How serious is the situation?" J.J. said.

"Holding them for now," Clay said. One of the bugs had managed to dodge the last swing, getting in close. Clay slammed his knee into the forehead of the thing's filthy face, ducked another's lunging charge, then hurled the creature he'd just dodged into the mansion's front wall. The crackly, stiff thing crumpled like a paper doll. "Three Harnesses are here though, and McGrath's with them. They'll probably engage as soon as I finish off the pack."

J.J. growled like a bear, his armor turning the sound into a thunderous digital rumble. "We'll get there before he engages, even if we overheat the hoverdrive doing it."

"Do what you've got to do, J.," Clay said.

"Always do," J.J. said. "We'll talk about this mess later. J out."

The line clicked, leaving Clay alone with the blood, bone, and screeches once again. As he continued to lash out, moving about like a young lion raging against a pack of filthy hyenas, he realized how tired he was growing. His lungs were working overtime, his reaction time turning slower and slower with each second that passed. He slipped on a loose corpse as he moved, stumbling and falling to the earth with a thud. No sooner had he hit the ground than he was tackled, assaulted by a gang of bugs, some of whom began to try and chew their way through his armor while others slammed rocks and fists into his head and arms. He elbowed one of the swarm in the face, kicked another, threw a third a few dozen feet in the air. Slowly but surely, struggling against the wave of crazed, deformed people, he arose, determination tangible in his grunts and battle cries. He glanced inside. Some of the infected had ceased their attack and were coming into the structure through windows and along the ceiling.

Time to retreat, he thought, his blood bursting through his body, his knuckles aching from colliding with a thousand skulls. He threw his improvised club like a spear, impaling a couple bugs, then slowly inched through the door and down the hallway as he continued to fight. They were on all sides of him now, above him and on the walls around him. He reached up, tearing a few from the ceiling and hurling them down the hallway in different directions.

I need my space, guys, he thought. The swarm continued to press in on him, kicking his claustrophobia into high gear.

Gunshots sounded in the basement, a few bullets punching through the floorboards, spraying bursts of green, infected blood into the air.

He scowled. *Guess the horde's downstairs now.*

He punted one bug and backhanded another, then plunged a hand into one of the surrounding walls, grabbed a support beam, and wrenched the wooden plank from its position. He spun the piece of wood like a spear, running it through the infected on all sides with its splintered ends.

His mind was whirring. He needed to keep the pressure off the basement, but he didn't know what he could do. The fastest way to get downstairs would be to punch through the floor, but he could collapse the whole basement if he tried. Worse still, he may be more of a problem than an aid if he got down there. A stray bullet could ricochet off him and hurt one of the other three in close quarters.

Gotta end this now and just deal with McGrath, he thought.

Then, as he flailed and thrashed at the surrounding throng, a bright, yellow beam blasted through the hallway, incinerating the bugs around him and sending him sprawling into the kitchen.

"McGrath," Clay grunted. Sure enough, McGrath hovered down through the hole in the ceiling he'd just made until his Harness floated just above the old, rickety floor.

Lucky there were all the bugs in the hall, Clay thought. *The bodies must've taken most of the blast.*

"You've looked better, Moore," McGrath said over the sounds of carnage. In spite of the death and insanity that surrounded them, McGrath's voice was as chipper and smiley as ever. "Armor's got blood all over it. Your usual look is definitely more flattering."

"Sorry," Clay said. "I'll make sure to clean up for our next appointment." In one motion, he stood, tore the kitchen's fridge from its place, then hurled it down the hall.

McGrath deflected the huge projectile easily with one of his optic blasts and chuckled. Then he was at Clay's throat, spanning the distance between them in an instant. Clay's feet came off the ground and then he was soaring through the kitchen wall and back out into the rain.

"No need to rearrange your wardrobe," McGrath said, floating through the hole in the wall. "This should be our last visit. Of course, we'll need to get rid of your buddies in the house. Can't have them causing more problems."

Two Harnesses appeared from behind the mansion, hovering feet above the house. The Harness with orange light coursing down its arms flared with passion. Massive flames flew from its hands, igniting the damp mansion.

Clay got up, ready to dive into the flames. No sooner had he taken a step than the Harness with indigo and white light flowing about it snapped, a purple bubble of solidified light materializing around Clay and trapping him inside its confines.

Clay slammed his fists into the transparent prison, pounding the colorful confines with all his might. Anxiety blocked everything else out for a second. It was just him and the barrier, which started pressing in on him incrementally.

They're going to suffocate me, he thought. He was short of breath already, his lungs heaving.

Get a hold of yourself, his training said. *Deep breaths. You're in control.* He pounded the barrier again, then kicked it with all the force he could muster.

"Oh, come on, Clay," McGrath said. "You know full well that'll do nothing. That field's too strong for you."

Clay rammed his shoulder into the barrier again and again. Bugs fell to the ground in front of him as the burning house scorched them, burning quickly in spite of the rain and the mud. Steam and smoke billowed as the fire . Clay snarled, ramming into the field time and time again.

Come on, Moore, his training told him. *Save the civilians. Step up, Vanguardsman.* He hit the barrier without ceasing, cracks forming in the wall. Then, before he realized, he broke through.

He didn't make it one step closer to the house. McGrath tackled him to the ground with brutal force and absolute efficiency the moment he burst through that wall. Clay's armor cracked on impact, the lines forming spider web patterns in the obsidian right in front of his eyes.

"Surprised you," Clay said.

"Yes, once again, Clay, you've surprised me," McGrath said, his foot firmly planted on Clay's neck. "For that exact reason, I've been given orders to execute you, here and now. Congratulations. You've been such a problem that you made the biggest bureaucracy in the history of the world decide to ditch standard protocol."

Clay's heart skipped a beat, his skin suddenly slick with sweat, but he did not say a word. He hit McGrath's legs from a number of angles, slamming the knee and battering the Harness's ankle joint.

"We can do this one of two ways," McGrath said. "You can come out of your armor and have a quick, easy death. One bullet to the head."

Clay heaved at McGrath's foot. "Or?"

"Or I can beat that armor off of you, break a few bones, then have you die slowly from internal bleeding," McGrath said. "You've got until the count of three to make your choice."

Clay clenched his jaw as he lay amidst the mud and blood, staring at the burning mansion. The fire licked hungrily at it, a ravenous scavenger devouring the wooden carcass. He battered the Harness's knee joint again.

"One," McGrath said.

Don't die on me, Clay thought. He scanned the house's façade, searching for any sign of Natalie, Dune, or Sage. He looked into every window, hoping for some sign of movement. There was none. His knuckles were bleeding now, the cracks in his obsidian grating against them.

"Two," McGrath said, his foot pushing a little harder into Clay's neck.

"Screw you, McGrath," Clay gasped.

McGrath skipped *three* altogether. Before Clay could try anything else, he was lifted over the large man's head, then came crashing back into the ground with unbelievable force. His armor's cracks grew longer and thicker, like roots working their way through his defenses. He felt a sharp, pulsing pain in his back, his spine protesting against the abuse as any air in him suddenly disappeared.

McGrath grabbed him by the head as he lay, coughing, amidst the bodies of the dead infected. "You're just a glutton for punishment, aren't you, Moore?" McGrath said. He slammed Clay's head into the mud twice. Clay gasped for air, his lungs still refusing to function correctly as McGrath stomped on the obsidian surrounding his head, each unstoppable blow pushing Clay into the earth beneath him. His obsidian armor splintered, pieces entirely disintegrating, though most of it withstood the blows. McGrath raised his foot again, relieving the pressure on Clay's head.

"Bye, Moore," he said. "Thanks for the excitement. It's been an adventure."

Clay tried to roll out from under the Chancellor, but the Harnessed foot fell too soon. Clay wasn't even thinking anymore. There was only the concentration and the force bearing down on him. He screwed his eyes closed, focusing as best he could. Another blow came, then another.

"Just die, Moore," McGrath hissed.

"Chancellor," one of the Harnesses said urgently.

"What?" McGrath said.

Clay heard a resounding thud, then a string of profanity from McGrath's lips.

"Evening, Chancellor," said a voice as vast, full, and cold as the wet, rainy night.

J.J., Clay thought, and his eyes opened. He struggled to look over the mound of dead infected between himself and his friend. McGrath's foot was now resting, protectively, on his neck once more. Then Clay saw him.

J.J. looked like some futuristic knight of heaven, his silver, glossy armor reflecting the light of the three Harnesses before him and the burning house behind them. He stood head and shoulders over all of them, a blazing, fiery sword brandished in one hand, a glowing, steaming shield on the other. Light shone from within his armor through one plate-sized circle on his chest and through his helmet's facemask, giving a small indication of the wrath and power contained within. Just above the heart, Clay could barely make out an engraving in the night. *Eccl 3:8*, it said.

"Hey, J," Clay said. The words barely made it through his lips.

"Get your foot off my boy, McGrath," J.J. said.

"My bad, Wright," McGrath said. His signature cheery voice had returned, no doubt trying to cover the fear within its bearer. "He didn't tell me he was 'your boy.'"

"Well, he is," J.J. said. "So, remove your foot."

McGrath chuckled as Clay felt the oppressive weight of the man's heel remove itself from his neck. "Of course, of course," he said.

The two sides attacked without any warning. One of McGrath's sidekicks, the one with the ability to create fire, rained a pillar of flame down on J.J.'s head. The hungry inferno burst downward, a geyser of heat and pain, but J.J. stood motionless in the face of it, his armor radiating with vicious light as the oppressive stream of heat passed over it. Then he moved, and it was as if a mountain had leapt forward. His gigantic shell of metal lunged, heaving over the heap of dead in a single bound, his sword of light at the ready, a beacon in the night. The earth shook when he landed, and his swing seemed to cut the very air. McGrath was forced to take to the sky, fleeing like a scared crow, chattering orders at his lackeys. Some of the wreckage and bodies took off into the air, obscuring J.J.'s view of his opponents.

Telekinetic, Clay thought disjointedly. He looked at the purple and white Harness. The war machine hung suspended in the air, arms folded as it controlled the movements of debris and flesh. The moving mass of inanimate objects and corpses fell suddenly, its telekinetic master crying out in shock as ice coated her armor like some cold, fast-acting weed.

"He's got help!" McGrath cried.

A projectile caught the struggling armor gleaming with purple and white in the small of the back, sending her crashing to the ground. The projectile stood after the two of them came to a stop, revealing itself to be a short, tough woman with short, brown hair. She pinned the significantly larger Harness, dealing punch after punch to its helmet until, eventually, it stopped moving.

J.J. was in continuous motion. His sword spun and twisted through the night as he fought, painting the air around him with radiant color like some lethal, solidified firework. Blast after blast of raging fire billowed around him, most staved off by his blindingly-bright shield. McGrath fired at him, dove to try and get a hit on him, then retreated, zipping away like a bird. J.J. parried, blocked, and dodged each attempt, each step calculated, each move planned. Then, with a too-fast-to-see-it swing, he threw his sword skyward, its blazing blade easily impaling the Harness whose armor shone in orange and blue. McGrath roared as his only remaining comrade slowly fell to the earth, lights flickering and armor melting around the burning blade. The Chancellor turned, ready to retreat into the night sky. However, the night sky refused to receive him, slowing him back with tornado-level winds. J.J. approached him leisurely, no doubt savoring the moment as McGrath desperately tried and failed to escape. Finally, J.J. grabbed his enemy by the ankle and flung him to the ground, pinning him with a huge, mechanical foot.

"He got him," Clay mumbled. "After all these years, he got him."

15

Natalie

Natalie smiled as the fight unfolded before her.

The three of them hid behind one of the many piles of dead bugs, Sage lying beside Natalie as they all watched the god-like soldiers go to war right in front of them. The blows rattled her teeth, the heat of the fire making her sweat.

This is the view I've been waiting for, she thought. *This is what I've lived for.*

Dune sighed beside her. She knew he wasn't as impressed. He'd seen dozens of these kinds of fights back during his Spec Ops days. Natalie, however, had not, so she settled in and enjoyed the view.

The combat was a blend of a professional MMA fight, a military battle, and a light show. Fire shot out in all directions. Harnesses blazed with color. Debris soared about, forming into some great appendage for one second, then exploding out into a swirling cyclone of garbage, then reforming into some new shape. The huge silver man with the blazing sword, the one Moore had called "J," stood in the midst of it all, lunging, jabbing, and blasting away at his enemies. Natalie had never seen anything like it. Kent had been a fascinating man to know. Some of her most peaceful moments in life were when she had watched him fly about, scouting areas in the morning. Even still, his wings couldn't measure up to the fireballs and forcefields these guys were flinging around.

"What do you think?" Dune asked.

"Shh!" she said. "It's almost over."

Sure enough, the giant armored in silver had the Chancellor in a bear hug, his fingers digging into the Harness's black plating.

"Let's go ahead and take your toy away," J said. He tore the Harness open with one titanic heave.

The Chancellor gasped, still trapped inside what remained of his Harness, though the armor fizzled and died around him. J tossed McGrath into one of the piles of bodies, then retrieved the sword he'd used to the Harness that had formerly blazed with orange and blue light. The sword's fire had slowly gone out, but it returned to its former flaming glory once it was back in his hand.

A few others had appeared out of the night. The smaller woman that had taken out the third Harness walked up as the Chancellor climbed out of the remains of his Harness, pushing the significantly larger man back into the pile of bodies. Another man appeared out of the night, coated in a thick layer of ice and some armor. A woman accompanied him, this one sporting slightly longer, dark hair that she kept back in a tight, neat bun. Though all were dressed in battle armor, none wore the Syndicate insignia.

Interesting, Natalie thought. *Wonder if all of Clay's friends are Vanguardsmen, or only some of them.*

McGrath stood, a tight, long sleeve shirt and some leggings acting as his only protection. Thanks to the woman's shoving, he was now covered in muck and at least a bit of infected blood. And yet, he stood tall, his shoulders squared and his chin up.

Say what you will about the Chancellor, Natalie thought. *He does keep a cool head.*

"It's been a while, Wright," McGrath said.

"It has," Wright, the massive mountain of armor, responded. "I think the last time I saw you was when you were on live television, executing my wife."

The Chancellor shrugged. "You were the highest-ranking officer in the Vanguard who escaped. You know I was just doing my job. Orwell wanted a message to be sent—I had to send it."

"What a waste of space you are," the short woman said.

"That's *opportunistic* waste of space, to you," McGrath said.

"Both of you, shut it," Wright said.

"What do you want, Wright?" McGrath said. "Revenge? Credits? A bargaining chip?"

"Oh, I just wanted Clay," Wright said. "You're a bonus."

"So, you're going to kill me, then," McGrath said. He stood defiantly, the misty rain drizzling down his well-built chest and arms.

"Oh, no," Wright said. He found Clay's unconscious body as he spoke, carrying the man in his arms like a child. "Your boss Orwell will do that for me."

McGrath's muscles tensed, a small wave of fear visibly rolling through his body.

How the mighty fall, Natalie thought, relishing in the sudden shift in the Chancellor's demeanor.

A forced laugh came from the man's lips. "You're going to leave me for him? He won't kill me—I've been too loyal. I'm too good at what I do."

"Obviously not," Wright said. He walked away, motioning toward the wasteland of the battlefield around him. The other Vanguardsmen followed him. "All these resources spent and how many so-called carriers did you bring in?"

"None tonight, but I've brought him plenty before," McGrath said. He followed the departing pack of super-humans, his composure evaporating. "What if I'm tired of it, though? All the killing and hunting? I could be an asset to you."

Wright said nothing. The short woman spat in McGrath's direction.

Natalie began to stand, but Dune grabbed her by the wrist.

"Where are you going?" he said.

She rolled her eyes. "Where do you think? They're our ride. Let go."

"They just became some of the Syndicate's most wanted criminals for sure," Dune said. "No way I'm going with them."

Natalie pulled herself free and started walking after the departing Vanguardsmen. "Stay if you feel like it, but I don't want to be alone here when the bugs come hunting again."

Sage was at Natalie's side in an instant, giving her a strained smile. *She really doesn't like the bugs,* Natalie thought.

She didn't look to see if Dune was coming. *Dune always comes.*

McGrath was still talking and Natalie could just hear him, though the other group was a ways ahead. "There's got to be something you want, Wright," he said. "I'll give you any intel you need. Just take me to a location of my choosing."

"McGrath, I don't make deals with the devil and, while you might not be the devil, you sure as hell work for him," Wright said. "You're not going anywhere with us."

"What about us?" Natalie cried out.

J's massive frame came to a stop, his big, metal head turning to get a look at her. "You the people that busted him out?" he said, holding up Clay's body.

"Yessir," Natalie said.

Sage waved.

Meets a Vanguard and all she does is wave, Natalie thought. *Who waves?*

Dune stood on the other side of Sage, looking positively miserable. *Oh, boo hoo,* Natalie thought. *Cheer up, Dune.*

"McGrath's men tried to burn us alive in the house," she said. "As you can see, that didn't work out, largely thanks to your intervention."

McGrath grimaced.

"Well, I appreciate your help," J said. "My name's J.J. Wright. All of you, follow me. We'll work something out with you, but I've got things to do and places to be."

A small skyship cruised downward, pulling up so fast Natalie nearly thought it'd collide with the unforgiving earth. Its hatch opened up and a ramp extended.

J.J. turned to the lot of them, arm extended toward the belly of the ship.

"Get on fast," he said. "The night's only just begun."

EPILOGUE

McGrath

McGrath was shivering, wet to the core by the time they picked him up, the misty Washington rain slowly seeping through the clothes he'd worn under his Harness. The warship descended from the cloudy night sky, the spotlights on its underbelly piercing the night like white pillars in a sea of space, homing in on the place where he sat on the burnt remains of the mansion's porch.

"Took them a while," he muttered. A landing craft descended from the ship like a small feeder fish detaching from a whale's belly.

He was silent as they took him up into the ship. There were no salutes, as there had been. They didn't handcuff him when they docked in the warship, but he wasn't led to the captain's quarters either. He was, instead, left in his tight, soggy attire and led to a basic officer's room. He now sat on the firm bed, his wet leggings slowly soaking the sheets beneath him.

How the mighty fall, he thought. He looked at the room's empty bookshelf and nightstand, his only companions, both absolutely useless.

According to the calculations the scientists had been running, under twenty-five Vanguardsmen were still out in the world. That meant he'd encountered one fifth of the Vanguard population tonight and had failed to incapacitate any of them.

He frowned. *Should've killed Moore*, he thought. *Should've finished him, then dealt with Wright.* He sighed, rubbing his hands together in frustration. He looked out the window, watching the North American continent pass by beneath the ship—forests, abandoned cities, and lakes zipping by like afterthoughts.

He still couldn't believe how empty it was. He hadn't been able to imagine it before Orwell had started the Outbreak and it still seemed so unreal to him. He'd visited the suburb he'd been raised in. Awful place just outside Savannah, Georgia, filled with stereotypical American houses. He'd hated it when he was a kid but, unbelievably, he hated it even more now. Hated its broken streets, its empty, leaning houses.

"This is the price we have to pay to save the world," he'd been told.

He hadn't believed Orwell's words back then, he certainly didn't believe them now. He'd never been with the Syndicate because he believed the ideology. He didn't know if Orwell even believed it. He was pretty sure the guy just wanted to be in charge and was smart enough to get himself there without the world throwing a fit about it. He watched as they zipped past the Rocky Mountains, stone giants pointing heavenward from below.

He turned away from the window, leaning against the wall beside it. He stared at the blank wall that stood opposite from the bed, then closed his eyes, leaning his head against the cool metal of the ship's frame behind him.

The door opened just as he was about to drift off into sleep. His eyes snapped open and his muscles tensed, wary and alert, only to immediately relax. "Hey, Clarkson. I didn't know you were running this ship."

The Syndicate captain took a seat on the metal nightstand that sat beside his bed, her arms folded. They didn't say anything for a few minutes, just stared at the blank room's walls. She spoke first.

"Word is, you're going to die tonight."

"I figured."

"You think the White Hart will do it himself?"

McGrath nearly rolled his eyes. He'd never liked Orwell's title, thought it was too weird and poetic. "Probably," he said. "Orwell likes to vent his disappointment at times like these."

Clarkson nodded. "They were a tough team, I'm guessing."

"The Vanguardsmen? Yeah, they were a strong squad. Well-coordinated, too. Led by an old acquaintance."

"The carriers, you mean?"

He did roll his eyes this time. "Yeah," he said. "The carriers."

"How many were there?"

"I saw five, total."

Clarkson nodded. "You think they'll cause problems?"

McGrath shrugged. "Maybe. I don't know. Won't bother me, either way."

Clarkson nodded, almost saying something more, but stopping herself short. "Well, good luck," she said. She turned for the door.

"Yeah, you too," McGrath said. His words just barely made it out through the closing door. He sat quietly a few moments after, then leaned back against the wall again.

Smart woman, he thought. She hadn't said anything personal, hadn't given anything away. She knew as well as he did that the rooms were all bugged. He'd understood the unstated message, though. She appreciated the help he'd given her when she'd been climbing the command ladder. She was sorry to see him go.

He closed his eyes again.

They landed minutes later. Skyships ran so smooth nowadays, he didn't even realize they'd touched down until his escort arrived at his room. Four Syndicate privates, all decked out in their plain, gray suits of armor, rifles at the ready.

"Welcome to Detroit, sir," the private in front said. "We'll take you to the White Hart."

"Well then, lead the way," McGrath said, standing from his bed.

They walked down the warship's ramp onto the White Tower's landing pad, the massive structure rising into the night sky in front of him. Architecturally, it was elegant. The whole structure was porcelain white, a building of smooth, graceful lines and curves. In a very real way, it symbolized its most famous resident: Nathan Orwell, the Syndicate's White Hart.

The city surrounding the tower was also very much an extension of Orwell. The buildings were clean, geometric, well maintained. The streets were surprisingly devoid of any form of garbage and the alleys were empty of any kind of stray pet or homeless person. Poverty didn't exist within its bounds, and everyone had their own home, their own roof, and their own view of the stars at night.

You'd never think people were starving just one city over, McGrath thought. *People don't even think about the hordes anymore. Orwell keeps them away from the city.*

The whole place bored him to tears. The administrative feel of it all, the sterility was entirely boring. Then again, the cutthroat political machinations of different residents were fun to watch, sometimes.

Get so many high-ranking politicians and administrators together, they're bound to try and off each other.

He missed the battlefields of the early days, though. The Harness-on-Vanguard fights. Plowing through hordes of Infected for the propaganda vids. That was what he'd signed up for. He'd enlisted for war.

And I got saddled with this, he thought as they walked through the tower's halls. His bare feet were cold against the milk-white marble floor. The white stone walls stood, elegantly, all around him. A quiet fortress in a far-too-quiet world.

They got halfway down the hall before he made his move, but once the move was made it was devastating. He pounced without warning, snapping the neck of one of the two guards in front of him, catching the man's firearm before it hit the floor, having fallen out of his now-limp hand. McGrath then opened fire on the other three, hiding behind the first guard's corpse. He knew he'd been escorted by so few soldiers because it was suicide to try anything inside Orwell's unofficial palace. Orwell would intervene within three seconds, killing the perpetrator.

Good thing I only need two seconds, McGrath said as all the soldiers fell dead. He ripped a hearlink out of the first guard's ear, then dropped the now-useless shield of a body. "Syndicate access code: One-nine-four-eight-one-one. Activate protocols one-three-four-eight and four-seven-seven-five-three. All systems go."

He stood still for a moment, time seeming to freeze as he waited for the protocols to go into effect. The palace rung with silence, the air thick with it.

Then the second passed. McGrath cursed.

He heard Orwell approaching before he could see the ruler dressed in white. McGrath didn't run. He wasn't stupid enough to think there was anywhere for him to go. Instead, he relaxed and turned to face his death.

The palace came apart as if it were assembled with toy blocks, the wires within the stone walls shifting to open a pathway for their master, the structure moved by the sheer might of Orwell's mind. He floated through the opening he'd made in the ceiling, descending from above like some god clothed in regal armor. The White Hart's Harness fit in amidst the white of his tower. Unlike all other Harnesses, the armor on him was pure white and emitted no light whatsoever. Instead, its alabaster surface was disturbed by a glossy black triangle located in the center of his facemask and another, somewhat larger triangle found in the center of the breastplate. Strips of white fabric flowed out of the armor's cracks and crevices, turning into a long, flowing cloak that spread like stolen angel wings as Orwell levitated.

The armor's color sent a powerful subliminal message. It and its bearer belonged in this tower. Everyone else was only a visitor.

"That was unnecessary," the White Hart said, "You got blood on the marble."

"I don't particularly care," McGrath said. His eyes wandered, unsure of where to look. The White Hart's entire face was covered in metal, no eyes to look into, to pierce with an angry stare.

I don't need a visor, the White Hart had always said. *I see through everyone else's eyes.*

"You believe this meeting is your execution," Orwell said.

"Of course I do," McGrath said, shoulders squared. "We've been working closely for how many years now? Twelve? Thirteen? I know you."

"If you truly knew me, Roy, you wouldn't have tried to use your two 'secret' protocols," Orwell said. "You should've known I would find them."

"True," McGrath said. "You never did trust anyone but yourself."

"And so far, that's been a good policy, wouldn't you say?"

McGrath shrugged. "It's not good for me, as we can both see. But, yeah, it's helped you well enough."

"Indeed, it has," the White Hart said, and McGrath felt the weight of the ruler's mind press against him. Its invisible, unbreakable grip wrapped around his body, locking his limbs in place.

"We'll speak for a moment before we part, though," Orwell said. They both floated through the air, back through the opening in the ceiling, and into Orwell's office. The building rebuilt itself behind them, the blocks and wires returning to their rightful place at the White Hart's unspoken command.

The room was more of a throne room than an office. Its commonly-used entrance was guarded by two massive white doors, each of which had a single raven engraved onto them. The wall facing the doors was lined with books, each of which the Hart had read long ago and each of which bore silky, white covers. McGrath had always thought the library was overkill. Almost no one read books these days. The cutting down of trees was illegal, books were generally inconvenient, and paper cuts were hellish. But, of course, exceptions could always be made for the unofficial king of the world.

A white chair rested in front of the bookcase, hovering over the ground, its overly-high back reaching up into the air. Then, in front of the chair, there stood a marble desk, with a large interface built into its top surface, giving the Hart constant access to whatever intel and information he desired. A lonely strip of white, silky grass-carpet extended from the desk to the doorway, marking the long walk it took to reach Orwell once anyone entered the chamber.

"I have to say, this occasion mildly saddens me, Roy," the Hart said as they hovered. "As you said earlier, you and I have been partners in our endeavors for some time now. It's regrettable that you've fallen like this. I've rather enjoyed relying on you."

"Feeling's not too mutual, Nate," McGrath said. "Working for you has sucked the last few years."

"I'm sorry to hear that, though I can't say I'm surprised. I expected a soldier like you to disappear from the ranks years ago."

"Nowhere to go, unless you expected me to leave for the front in Africa."

"True enough," Orwell said. He set McGrath down in front of the desk as he set himself in his white throne. They sat in silence for a few moments, the White Hart presumably staring silently at McGrath from within his faceless armor.

"What do you want, Orwell?" McGrath said. "Why not just kill me?"

"I'm curious," Orwell said. "Are you ready to die? Are you afraid?"

"I thought you could read my mind, Orwell. You've got your answer."

"There's something different about hearing you say it, Roy," Orwell said. His voice sounded slightly hungry, craving the answer.

"I don't love the thought of it, Nate."

"And yet, you're so peaceful."

"Nothing I can do will change the fact that I'm going to die," McGrath said. "No point in worrying about it now."

"There's the McGrath practicality I know and love," Orwell said. His cool voice sounded happy. Far too happy.

"Now I'm curious, Orwell," McGrath said. "What do you think of death?"

The White Hart, ruler of the world and killer of billions, leaned his head back and laughed. "Oh, my dear Roy," he said once he was done, "What a stupid question. I'm never going to die."

And with that, he killed McGrath.

The Departure

Mason Allan was raised traveling throughout the world. He spends his time in a myriad of ways, but he's always dreaming and thinking up new ideas. He enjoys eating new foods and has recently tried eating the spicier stuff he's avoided for most of his life. Currently, Mason is working on the rest of the Rebellion series, in addition to three other projects he hopes to release in coming years. Feel free to follow his journey on Twitter. His handle is @mrmasonallan.

Made in the USA
San Bernardino, CA
23 August 2019